**Adel Kamel** (1916–2005) was an Egyptian novelist, short story writer, and playwright. He was a founding member of the informal "harafish" writers' collective that included such eminent writers as Nobel laureate Naguib Mahfouz and Salah Jahin. He was considered to be at the vanguard of his generation, leading the push toward realism in Arabic literature. Despite the brevity of Kamel's career—*The Magnificent Conman of Cairo* (published in Arabic as *Malim al-akbar* in 1942) was his final novel—many critics and writers have recognized the importance of his legacy as a radical writer and, in 1993, Mahfouz took responsibility for reprinting his works.

**Waleed Almusharaf** is a translator, writer, and academic, and holds a PhD from SOAS, University of London. He translates both fiction and nonfiction, everything from Quranic exegesis to literary works, and his writing has been published in a number of outlets, including *Mondoweiss* and *Mada Masr*. He currently lives in California in the United States.

# The Magnificent
# Conman of Cairo

## Adel Kamel

Foreword by

### Naguib Mahfouz

Translated by

### Waleed Almusharaf

**hoopoe**

AN IMPRINT OF AUC PRESS

First published in 2020 by
Hoopoe
113 Sharia Kasr el Aini, Cairo, Egypt
200 Park Ave., Suite 1700, New York, NY 10166
www.hoopoefiction.com

Hoopoe is an imprint of the American University in Cairo Press
www.aucpress.com

Dar el Kutub No. 11978/19
ISBN 978 977 416 967 0

Dar el Kutub Cataloging-in-Publication Data

Kamel, Adel
        Mallim al-Akbar / Adel Kamel.— Cairo: The American University in
Cairo Press, 2020.
        p.  cm.
        ISBN 978 977 416 967 0
        1.  English fiction
        2.  English literature
        823

1 2 3 4 5    24 23 22 21 20

Designed by Adam el-Sehemy
Printed in the United States of America

# Adel Kamel, the Harafish, and Literature

*By Naguib Mahfouz*

IN THE EARLY 1940s, A generation of writers got to know one another. Our group consisted of Adel Kamel, Abdel-Hamid Gouda al-Sahhar, Ali Ahmed Bakthir, Mahmoud Badawi, Youssef Gohar, Hussein Afifi, and Ahmed Zaki Makhlouf. They were all at the beginning of their literary lives, and Adel Kamel was at the vanguard: brilliant and doing exceptional work. It was a single generation in the same place and from the same background, and it's no surprise that a critic would find that they shared ideas, orientations, and styles.

As for me, from the moment we met as writers, Adel invited me to join the Harafish, a writer's collective. At the time, the members were Adel himself, Zaki Makhlouf, and Ahmed Mazhar. There were also Amin al-Zahaby, Thabet Amin, Mahmoud Shabana, Asem Helmi, and others who are now deceased, may God have mercy on them. Later, we were joined by Tawfiq Saleh, Mohamed Afifi, and Salah Jahin, as well as, occasionally, Ahmed Bahaa, Louis Awad, and others.

In terms of writing, Adel Kamel was ahead of us in that he had already had his work published: *Wake Up, Antar (Wayk*

*Antar)*, which he published himself, and then *The Magnificent Conman of Cairo (Malim al-akbar)*, and *King of Light (Malik min al-shu'a')*. But, beginning in 1945, he began to have doubts. He doubted the role of literature and the point of art as a whole. All his conversation began to revolve around this one point, such that, had his influence on us become complete, we might all have abandoned literature once and for all.

And then, to our surprise, he really did stop writing. For a long time we tried to argue him out of this strange position, urged him to continue, until, as I remember, he became angry. He asked us not to remind him of his decision. We considered it a personal issue, and we never did come to know the cause of it. Our guess, and it was a guess, was that he did not get the recognition he deserved, and that he was terrified of wasting his life. He fled to the practice of the law, and made a decent living out of this profession. From that day until today, as I write this, we assumed that he was done with writing forever. We were surprised then, later, to discover that he had written other works: unpublished manuscripts whose dates were not known. It came to light, also, that one of us, Tawfiq Saleh, did in fact know of the existence of these manuscripts and the dates of their writing, for he used to visit Adel privately in the 1960s and he would see him writing. This was the last period, it seems, that he wrote, and after this he stuck strictly to his profession. When we asked Adel why he did not publish them, despite having written them, even he did not know the answer, and his memory today seems to have lost its grasp on that time, so that the details are unclear even to him.

There seems to be no possible clear explanation for why a writer, suddenly and for all time, stops writing. I remember that such a condition came upon me once in 1952. I told my colleagues that I was done as a novelist, and that I would become a screenwriter. Years passed, and then, when I returned to writing novels, I simply said to my friends that things were now moving again. There seem to be reasons—for fleeing writing, for returning to writing—that even the writer doesn't know. I had, for example, inspiration: there were things to be written. I simply had no desire to write them. It was not an issue of being barren for me, nor do I recall that Adel ever complained of barrenness. What he thought, simply, was that writing literature was a useless thing.

In any case, Adel Kamel, as a fellow writer, is someone who has earned my utmost respect. As a friend, I count him as someone to whom I am very close. Since that day we met in 1943 there has been nothing but love and intimacy between us. When I found out that he had old work that would appear now, I had a longing: perhaps this was a sign that he would, once again, write.

*Cairo, 1993*

# Part 1

# 1

MALIM SAID, "NO DOUBT." THEN he picked up his tools and set off without a backward glance, determined, like a conqueror.

His friend just stood there with a mocking smile on his face. When Malim was a stone's throw away, his friend called out after him: "We'll see."

He said this, laughed, and set off down a different path.

The discussion between Khaled and his father reached an extreme. This was always the case whenever Khaled and his father had talked. No matter how small, how insignificant the matter at hand, the natural course of events was that any conversation would inevitably develop into a bloody battle between father and son.

Of course, Khaled's father was a wily son of a bitch. He took the kind of pleasure in power that drives a cat to play awhile with its prey before consuming it whole. He dragged his son into interminable arguments. He carefully steered the conversation toward ideas he knew full well his son would find utterly unbearable. He watched with a focused and malicious joy as his son's chest swelled with righteous rage and his face constricted with anxiety and discomfort.

No sooner had the poor boy rallied than he answered his father, saying, "No doubt."

Then he departed, rushing to the study and closing the door behind him.

Had he waited a moment longer, he would have seen that malicious smile on Ahmed Pasha Khorshed's face, and heard him say, "We'll see."

As soon as the Pasha said those words, he straightened his posture, thrust out his chest, and let loose from the depths of his throat a growling cough. He always did this when he determined to leave his home, as fair warning to all present that the master of the house was departing. Perhaps he was convinced that a cough like this would strike fear into them, as he repeated it when he arrived back at the house. And, in fact, on any occasion worthy of causing fear and trembling.

The moment his servant heard the official farewell cough, he ran to his master and handed him his cane. Then he raced to the door, opened it, and stood at military attention until the lord of the manor stepped over the threshold.

When Ahmed Pasha alighted on the path running through the mansion's gardens, the gardener and his assistants hurried to create a long line for him to stroll past with a scrutinizing gaze and an expression of profound grandeur.

Upon reaching his car—provided, of course, by the state—the soldier near its open door struck a military pose, body taut and holding a dignified salute.

With this, the morning performance was complete. The car transported Ahmed Pasha Khorshed to his place of work, for the beginning of the next performance.

Approximately one hour after the Pasha's departure from the manor, Malim was climbing the stairs of that stately home, filled with fear and trembling. He hesitated a long time. Then he rang the doorbell. The door opened, and a Nubian servant emerged and examined him for a long moment, and then said, "What do you want?"

Malim answered with a stutter, "I'm the carpenter's apprentice. I'm here to fix the window."

The servant cast a look of utter contempt on Malim's lowly self and asked, with a curl of his upper lip, "Why did your master not come himself?"

"He's sick today, and anyway, I can fix it just fine."

At this, the Nubian launched into a tirade against the Arabs and heaped upon them all the insults found in the unique language of his people. After some time had passed, he commanded Malim to remain in the garden until he was called upon. And so Malim sat in the shade of a tree, placed his tools next to him, and let his thoughts wander.

One thing was clear: this was not a good day. And he'd had such high hopes for it. It was, after all, the first day his master had entrusted him with a job. But Malim knew that life was nothing but struggle. It simply would not do to lose the will to fight. Not after he had steeled himself to refuse the life of a vagabond and layabout. He had to hold firmly to the belief that he was capable of treading the difficult path of honorable work.

Nevertheless, these little shocks disturbed him. He had been raised in the embrace of an absolute freedom, without limits—not even the limits of the law. And he was new at this, having left his previous life less than two months prior to this very moment.

In the neighborhood of Housh Eisa, he would leave his father's house in the early morning accompanied by his dog, Fido, and would not return before midnight. He inherited this style of living from his father except that his father did not have a dog. It was a life that wasn't tied to any home in particular. His father was not the lord of any domicile. Malim neither depended on his father, nor owed him obedience.

But perhaps there were some limits after all. Twice during the day, father and son would join forces on an enterprise that was their main livelihood.

Malim's father did not have a name like normal people. People simply called him the Madman of Housh Eisa. All that people knew about him was that he had, once upon a time, worked at a failure of a newspaper, where he seemed to have written their editorials and all the articles. He was not exactly a literary man. His level of literacy could be likened, say, to that of a ticket inspector on the tram. But he knew some odd facts about politics and some anecdotes about the lives of certain well-known politicians, and that was more than enough, since no one read his articles anyway. And in any case, the point of the articles was not to be read, but to fill the pages not filled by legal-notice advertisements. For the true mission of the paper, the service it provided the Egyptian people, was to present the public with these notices and in this way to broaden people's social horizons. Valuable knowledge was disseminated concerning the sales of calves and cows, and the seizure of land and real estate.

Nor were the duties of the Madman of Housh Eisa limited to editorial work. He was also responsible for distribution, of which he made a fine art. Despite the fact that the newspaper had no material worth reading, he managed to sell dozens of copies. He did this with his natural gifts: a silver tongue, a charming wit. Qualities that caused hearts to soften and hard currency to appear. However, the newspaper eventually disappeared. It disappeared the moment the government that the owner supported disappeared. At that point, the Madman set aside editing and focused all his attention on the fine art of distribution. Although what he distributed was no longer newspapers.

"Cool water, gardens, and a beautiful face!"

The Madman's voice rang out with these words every dawn and every afternoon as he arrived at a famous café in the neighborhood of al-Hussein. The café's customers would lift the stems of their hookahs from their mouths, turn toward him, and see him standing on the road. He would be wearing a dazzlingly white galabiya, with his basket in his hand and Malim by his side. The man was extraordinarily well dressed. Every day he would be wearing an immaculate galabiya different from the one he'd worn the day before. He would henna his hair. He doused himself in fragrant perfumes. His fingers were covered in gold rings. He always seemed like a groom on his wedding night. As for Malim, he never much cared about what he was wearing, but he had about him a regal quality that made him beloved to all who laid eyes on him.

After the Madman let loose his cry, he began to circulate among the tables. Whenever he met a group of young men, he swayed toward them, speaking intimately. "Beauty has made itself known. Lights have dawned upon us. Let us ornament it with some fragrant flowers." And he would grab a handful of flowers from his basket and distribute them, or scatter them over their clothes. The boys, eager to keep him by their side, would ask playfully, "What's the news, Madman?"

And here the Madman would divulge the latest secrets in the world of Egyptian politics. Private meetings between this luminary and that and all that was said in intimate detail. He would assure them that his information came from a trustworthy source, who had been present at that very meeting.

And then he would lean in close, shyly, and ask, "Can any of you fine young gentlemen spare a piaster for Malim?"

That was his approach with the young men. With the grown men and the old men, he had a different sort of discourse, which more often than not ended in him slipping them a small item wrapped in silver paper. The Madman was happy with this life, which afforded him many luxuries for little struggle. Malim too was content, because it afforded him absolute freedom. It saved him from the exhausting labors other boys of his age were forced into. How he disdained and lamented those poor souls whose fathers sent them to follow disintegrating carts piled high with pitiful merchandise. Chickpeas. Peanuts. Wandering endlessly along the roads in blazing summer and frostbitten winter, to return at the end of the day with pennies insufficient to feed or clothe anyone. And this if they didn't suffer, as they usually did, from the cruelty of the police, and the tyranny of statutes and laws that seemed to have been laid down for no reason but to block any way for the poor to make a living.

This was why it was necessary for the poor to break the law, or so it seemed to Malim. As for the rich, well, their police records were always clean. Malim felt simultaneously contemptuous and rebellious whenever he passed a police station and found a long line of street sellers and their carts rounded up by the police to be jailed or fined for their laboring to make a legitimate livelihood.

If the cops were not fond of these legitimate enterprises . . . well, there was another side to every coin. And Malim's father was a champion of that other side, which made the son a true admirer of his father. He was, in a word, his role model.

Of course, this other side required a careful attitude, a sharp wit from its adherents. Otherwise, you might find yourself face to face with those same cops. A catastrophic eventuality. What's more, some of those policemen were themselves champions of that other side of the coin. And that particular type of policeman had large hands.

Malim's father was diligent in shaking those hands from time to time. One day, however, a disagreement broke out between him and a cop, and the result was that he was gently deposited in prison. The crime he was accused of was suitably broad and distasteful. He was a guest of the security establishment long enough that he gained some weight, and the henna faded from his hair and moustache. And so Malim found himself without a father. He also found himself without an occupation to satisfy his needs. His friend Bunduq, with whom he had much in common, was of the opinion that he should complete the mission he inherited from his father: to bring joy to people with fragrance and flowers.

But Malim had grown tired of that kind of life. He was, of course, still in the flower of his youth, and he had started to feel a great desire to labor and strive, to expend his energy, to make an honorable living. He was at this point almost a man. He felt in his bowels a great energy, an agitation, which was unfamiliar to him. But he felt that this energy would have no outlet, no realization, if he continued on the path of "a piaster for Malim, gentlemen." Enough of that side of the coin. Let him try the side filled with statutes and laws. And that was why Malim steeled his will toward honorable work.

*

One day, his friend Bunduq met him hurrying down the road, in a straight path, leaning neither one way nor the other, and carrying a bag full of tools. He stopped him.

"What's this, Malim?" he asked.

"Tools."

"Are you picking a lock?"

"Actually, I am going to fix one. I am working at my uncle's workshop now."

"Oh yeah? And what does this uncle do?"

"He's a carpenter."

Bunduq's jaw dropped, and stayed dropped for some time. "A carpenter! A carpenter? Seriously? No. No. It can't be. I won't believe it."

Malim shrugged, and began to walk again. "Believe whatever you want—that's not my problem."

"And you're just going to be a carpenter? Forever?"

Malim turned to him, and there was a gleam of anger in his eye. Then he said, with some menace, "Do you have something against carpenters?"

"No, no, certainly not," Bunduq said with a laugh. "Nothing wrong with carpenters. But that's what they call honorable work. What I mean is: will it last?"

And here Malim cried out passionately: "No doubt!"

Bunduq cracked up, and said, "We'll see."

He said this and went on his way.

# 2

As soon as Khaled settled a bit, he reclined in a comfortable chair and let his thoughts roam.

Why was it that young men like him came and went, worked and raised hell, while he was alone in this room, going nowhere, doing nothing? His long meditations on himself had led him to the conclusion that he was precisely half a man. For the human being in general is a rational and a social animal. And while he had not yet lost his rational faculty, he could by no means be considered a member of society. He was alone.

How did this happen? he wondered. Was this tragic situation the result of a mistake he had made? Or had he been forced into it by the vicissitudes of fate? Usually, he figured it was fate. A cruel and unjust fate at that. Recently, however, it seemed to him that to blame fate was a way of deflecting, of excusing the faults of the self. Now he was convinced that the laws of nature produced its end products only by a vicious cycle of cause and effect. If society had rejected him, it was because he also rejected society, refusing its order and its conditions. Society embraced those who accepted the social order, and cleared the paths of success and progress for them. If society deemed acceptable, say, lies and bribes and fraud, well, there was no way an individual could succeed without accepting the validity of those methods. If the individual rebelled against those means, society rebelled against him, and he lived destitute, wretched. And rational.

It was a vicious cycle. He knew that God did not change the condition of a people until they changed what was in themselves. And yet, there seemed only two options, both equally bad. On the one hand, he could change society, shape it according to his desires. This was, of course, impossible. On the other hand, he could change himself, shape himself to conform to what society desired. This was even more impossible, for he was young, living in a world of words and meaning.

He wondered now who began these hostilities: was it him or society? Before he had traveled to Europe he was happily living with his family. He was a full member of the family and of society as a whole. He remembered laughter when they ate together. He remembered accompanying his mother and brother on visits to relatives and friends.

But when he completed his secondary education, his father sent him to a prestigious university in England. The first year passed peacefully. The world to him was still that tiny demographic: friends and family. All that concerned him personally were his sexual instincts and the desire for success. At the end of that year, however, he left England on a vacation that took him through most of the countries of Europe.

Khaled saw many things during that trip. As he was moving from place to place, he simply did not have the time to actually think about anything he saw at the time. But when he returned, his mind began to turn over what he had experienced and felt. And all this aggressive thinking was of course accompanied by some comprehensive psychological turmoil. He could not sleep. His head felt like a volcano, on the verge of eruption. He didn't know what shores he would be cast upon by the power of this eruption. At this point, Khaled's thoughts tended to drift from the specific to the general. His world was no longer composed of unique individuals; now it was divided into social classes. He began to see the rich and the poor in a different way. They were no longer the results of a whimsical, insensitive destiny that handed out wealth and poverty to whomever it willed. Wealth and poverty were now the necessary results of the precise interactions between political and economic systems.

And now, Khaled felt a great desire to read books. He consumed them. He would not let a book out of his grasp until he had finished with it completely, even if this came at the cost of his sleep or his meals. At the beginning of this era, he read anything he could get his hands on. But soon he had abandoned literature and poetry, and focused exclusively on historical monographs, economic research, and sociology. He became extremely impatient with fiction. He disliked how it ran rampant in the minds of men. What he wanted was the essence of those material truths controlled by the laws of nature. Those were things you could find the source of through diligent investigation. The effects of those truths could be teased out scientifically. There appeared before him a whole new world, and he wanted to know everything there was to know about it. What need then did he have for the wildness of imagination or the delusions of poets?

These psychological tendencies of his were encouraged by his general milieu. His college was filled with young English students who considered their country to be the champion of the global intellectual renaissance. They saw themselves as the vanguard, burdened with wielding the banner of progress toward modernity.

They wore themselves to the bone embracing the latest philosophical opinions and cutting-edge scientific theories. So it was no surprise that materialism reached them, and that it found in them the best of allies and the most zealous missionaries.

Three years passed, and Khaled read and listened and thought deeply. Then he got his degree and returned to Egypt. But the person who returned to Egypt bore no resemblance to the shy young man who had left the country just a few years earlier. If he were given a choice, he would have chosen his earlier self. He'd been happy then. He'd been content with everything. But he returned a sad and bewildered young man. He had lost his previous self, but was unable to find another. The intellect with which he returned couldn't see past its own nose. It had demolished an ancient and venerable structure, and had built in its place a little hut constructed with fragile supports. True, it was a pretty hut, but he didn't discern in it any tendency toward longevity. It was at best of some utility to a generation or two, and after that . . . come what may.

Khaled returned to Egypt in a frenzy of revolt against society as a whole. As soon as he settled in upon his return, his rage encompassed the entirety of that little microcosm of society: his family. He found them intolerable: his father, his older brother, and his mother, in that order of priority.

Before his departure he had felt toward his father that traditional respect he had felt since his infancy. It never occurred to him to question his orders or criticize his actions. He had left him when he was Ahmed Bey Khorshed, one of the most prominent judges in the country. When he returned, he found that his father had become Ahmed Pasha Khorshed, who must have come to occupy a truly dangerous position, since the state placed one soldier in front of his door during the day, and another during the night. This aura of authority did not inspire respect in Khaled. Rather, he found himself looking at his father with the kind of disapproving gaze that is capable only of revealing flaws.

Ahmed Pasha Khorshed grew up in the kind of family that led to a name like that. His father had no other sons but him. He had daughters, older than Ahmed, and so it was no surprise that Ahmed grew up spoiled, a little tyrant. He was aware that he was the favorite of everyone in his family, and that awareness never left him. He considered himself to be fashioned from a different clay than regular humanity. He could not bear any criticism or objections. His lot in life was to command; the lot of others was to obey. He was possessed entirely by this attitude, so that belittling people and impressing upon them their own inferiority became his main occupation. It seemed to him also that the laws governing the lives of other people simply were not relevant to him. It was the same feeling that artists and poets have, and which makes them feel entitled to destroy the chains of conventional thought and let their imaginations roam free. The same feeling that allows them to create *The Quatrains*, and *The Divine Comedy*, and *Hamlet*. All it did for Ahmed Pasha Khorshed was make him feel entitled to strip others of their rights, to permit him always to place his interests before others', and generally to consider nothing but himself.

Khaled had heard, to name but one example, a rumor spread by his father's enemies (and they were many). He could not verify it, but he had heard that his grandfather had been struck down by a terrible illness and that, when Ahmed Pasha sensed that the end was nigh, he visited him on his deathbed demanding more than his rightful share of the inheritance. It seems that his demands were rejected or not taken seriously, for, the rumor went, he waged a veritable war against his father. Day and night he raged against him, with the old man begging for mercy, and appealing to his weak condition and the pain he was in. As part of this campaign, he exiled his sisters from their home, to make certain they could not influence

18

the old man's decision. In this way, the old man found himself facing the specter of death alone, with no companions to wipe his feverish brow or wet his parched throat. And then one day, the old man's body was found at the bottom of the stairs, with several cracked ribs and a broken skull.

Some said that he had woken in the middle of the night in need of something or other, lost the way, slipped, and tumbled down the stairs. Other people said other things. When Khaled went to visit his grandfather's old house, and he saw the place the old man fell from, he understood why his aunts never set foot inside their brother's house, except for funerals. Even if his grandfather had slipped, it would have been impossible for him to fall in such a way as the stairs were flanked by a high railing.

After his return from England, Khaled had no doubt that his father had driven his grandfather to suicide. For he began to see how not a single day passed when his father did not prey on some victim. He dismissed his servants under the thinnest pretexts, and then kept their wages for himself instead of giving them severance pay. He sued the farmers to whom he leased land, and took their property, confiscating their money and selling their homes, seizing the very clothes off their backs. He released his dogs on trespassers, and the dogs would tear at their clothing with their teeth. Khaled heard that he flogged any peasants on his estate who happened to displease him. His cruelty became a thing of legend, and an unpleasant rumor spread that his greed must have come from a Jewish grandfather of his who loaned for interest, and who only became a Muslim to add prestige to wealth.

Ahmed Pasha Khorshed did not have friends. His dealings with his colleagues did not inspire affection. He shook hands with the very tips of his fingers, he accepted no chewing tobacco offered to him, and he did not respond to invitations for coffee. During his tenure as a judge, he had one glass and one coffee cup that he drank from. His fellow judges would recount how, while he perused the files of a case, he kept beside him a bottle of cologne, and how after turning each page, he would dip his finger in the cologne to cleanse it of any impurities. They also told the story of how one time, as he presided over a case, the defending attorney felt thirsty and asked for some water, which he quickly drank. Ahmed Pasha barked his surprise, asking incredulously, "How could you drink from that glass?" The lawyer glanced from the judge to the glass and back again. After a while he ventured, "It seems clean enough, Your Honor." The judge responded, "Clean enough? Clean enough? Young man, if I could wash water, I would!" In fact, even as a young lawyer himself, he had lost an important case by remarking to the judge that if he could, he would clean the air before inhaling it. For Khaled, there was no better expression of his father's ill-humored intolerance and the ugliness of his arrogance than that expression: "If I could wash water, I would."

This washer of water found his son, when he came back to him, to be a mess: disheveled, his clothing of low quality, unironed, dirty, and tattered to boot. It seemed likely that not only did the owner of these clothes not show them any mercy, but that he did not even let them rest when he slept. The father struck his forehead but he did not despair. He gave his son the benefit of the doubt. Perhaps the boy had chosen clothes appropriate for the rigors of travel. But when his luggage was opened, it revealed nothing but books. Books, antiques, and some gifts.

"Do you have nothing else to wear?"

"No."

That brief interview was the parting of the ways between father and son. From that moment, a protracted conflict began between them. Khaled really did try at the beginning, driven by innocence and lack of experience, to convince his father of some of the reformist theories that filled his head to the brim. Ahmed Pasha Khorshed listened to his son for a while. Then he interrupted him sharply. "You're a damned fool," he said. "A government of the people that you are talking about is the closest thing to bending over in front of an ass and asking *it* to ride *you*. Me, I like to ride my ass, not the reverse. You damned fool. I regret spending money on your education. It's gone on something worse than wine or women."

These discussions always ended with Khaled retreating and ceding the room to his father. Often, this was the dining table, which resulted in Khaled eating his dinner in his bedroom, to the point that this became the rule rather than the exception.

Ahmed Pasha thought his son would see the light, as soon as the fire died that drives the immature thinking that rules a young man's mind during his period of study. After all, such thoughts always died when a young man faced the prospect of making his way in the world. But the days passed, and turned into months, and it did not seem that Khaled was reconsidering. Indeed, he went even further astray, joining a group of his peers whose way of thinking gave Ahmed Pasha an ominous chill.

The man was genuinely afraid for his son. It did not seem that he gave a damn about the opinions of his father, nor did he have any respect for his father's desires. He feared his son's declaration of war, and, since Ahmed Pasha was not exactly known for his noble character, he opted for a preemptive strike. And so, one day, he walked into the room and found his son reading.

"You do not stand out of respect when your father walks in?"

"I didn't hear you knocking, Father."

"Don't use that kind of language with me, young man! With what do you occupy yourself?"

"Reading."

"The time for reading is over. Now is the time for work."

"The time for reading will continue as long as books are published."

"Nice. Do you think you got that degree to show it off in cafés with your friends?"

"I don't understand."

"Tomorrow morning you will go down to the Ministry of Foreign Affairs. I have found you a job with the minister."

"I don't really have any interest in the minister, and I don't think the minister cares much about me either."

"You mean you won't take the job?"

"My presence at the ministry is not likely to have much of an effect on Egypt's relations with other countries, I'm afraid."

"And are Egypt's relations with other countries improved by your lounging around my house unoccupied?"

"I'm not unoccupied. I'm reading."

"We'll see if you're occupied or otherwise when your allowance is cut off."

And the allowance was cut off. But Khaled did not quit his lack of employment. He reveled in it. No one could see upon him any effect whatsoever resulting from this maneuver, except that he spent even more time in his room, day and night, whereas he had passed brief amounts of time out of it before.

His mother came to him, weeping. She begged him to go to his father and seek forgiveness.

"Leave me alone, Mother," he said to her. "I'm no longer a little boy."

She cried out in grief. "What will people say? You have been struck by the evil eye! Come to your senses, my son!"

"What I would like," Khaled replied, "is for all of you to come to your senses for once. But you always return to your superstitions, your ignorance, and your selfishness."

At this point his mother began to talk more about evil-doers and sinners, and asking God to have mercy on His servants, and to return them to the path of righteousness. She then moved on to listing the types of calamities that had recently befallen the world. She insisted that the sole cause of said calamities was people's moral corruption.

"Enough, Mother. Your husband has arrived."

He knew if he let her keep going down this road, there would be no end to the journey, but he heard his father's official fatherly cough, and knew at least he wouldn't have to hear his mother's unbearable tragic recital to its very end. This seemed to have become her specialty. For some reason, she had developed the belief that she was now a saint, and had been chosen to advise everyone on how to live an ethical life. And so, every now and then, she filled the house with woeful cries.

"Save your servants, O Lord." There would be a brief silence. Then: "Raise Your wrath from us, O Lord!"

And so on. The servants no longer had any need to ask where their mistress was; all they had to do was follow the cries and wails. Between his father and his mother, Khaled could no longer bear the house, which he began to refer to as the House of Coughs and Wails. Nor was he the only one who hated the mansion. His mother's friends had ceased to visit. As for his father, he didn't have any friends.

When war failed, Ahmed Pasha resorted to appeasement. One day, Khaled saw an elegant automobile in the garden. He was told it was at his disposal. He woke up one morning and found his room filled with fashionable shoes and shirts of all designs and colors. One evening it was a stack of cash, seductive, tempting him with distant horizons. After all, Khaled, despite his antics, was still a healthy, red-blooded young man. A month passed, and then his father came in and said with a placating laugh, "My son! You are a man of deep thought and well-considered opinion. You are passionate about your message. But Khaled the unknown young man is not the same as Khaled who occupies an important position and has a wide influence. People only listen to those who command respect. Be Khaled the minister! Khaled the general director! Do this, and then say what you will. Pearls of wisdom or horse manure, whatever you want, and you will find that people follow you. If you do as I advise you, and take the job I have lined up for you, you will be furthering your message and taking practical action to achieve your goals."

Khaled found himself convinced by these words. He began to say to himself, "Oh, you have it right this time, Pasha. But you missed one thing. You forgot to say that this job will free me from my dependence on you. It will allow me to cast off the shackles of this household once and for all. That's why I'll take the job, Pasha!"

But despite being optimistic about the job on his first day, he left work increasingly depressed. He was filled with disgust. It was the kind of disgust he had felt only once before, just a month previously. The kind of disgust he had felt in that car when he had known a woman's body for the first time in his life. In both cases his imagination had collided with reality, and in both cases Khaled had felt a profound contempt for his own self. For allowing it be degraded in this manner. He felt dirty.

When he first presented himself to his colleagues at the ministry, he noticed how they greeted him with a smile he did not quite understand. They sat him down in a comfortable chair, and began to ask him about his health, the Pasha's health. They ordered coffee for him and offered him cigarettes. He refused all these offers, not only out of boredom but because there was something about it all he didn't quite understand.

Things continued like this for some time. After a while, he gathered his courage and asked them for the work he was supposed to be doing. Their smiles widened. The meaning of these smiles was something like this: "What work, little boy? The likes of you, who arrive every now and then, are not here to do any kind of work!"

He insisted. They gave him an enormous folder, and told him it was the paperwork concerning such and such a treaty, which was finally concluded after so many years of arduous negotiation. His job was to sort out the contributions His Excellency the new minister had made to the treaty.

Khaled took the folder with some distaste. It seemed to him that they were assigning him the type of work parents sometimes gave their children when they wanted them out of their way: tantamount to counting the pages of a book, say, or building sandcastles. Despite this, he delved into the folder. He read through the papers for an hour or a bit more, and then he raised his head and said, "The new minister contributed absolutely nothing to these negotiations."

"It doesn't matter," they answered.

"Let's assume for a moment," Khaled remarked, "that I actually did this work. What exactly would be the point of it?"

"It would be material for an article we would send to a newspaper to publish."

"And I will not be the one writing it."

And he got up and left.

He cocooned himself in his room for a week after this incident. And then he went to the ministry. He met his colleagues with a smile that mirrored theirs, and sat in his comfortable chair for half an hour, during which time he read the newspaper, then excused himself and departed. He knew now that he could face those bureaucrats without shame. There was no difference between them and himself except that they were ignoramuses and hypocrites. The ignorant were those employees who toiled day and night on labor that brought the country no benefit. The hypocrites were those colleagues of his who merely pretended to work. As for himself, well, if he neither worked nor gave the appearance of work, that only made him better than them, since at least he saved the state the cost of the stationery he would otherwise have used.

One day he took a brief tour of the offices in the ministry. He found that there were three types of work being carried out in the building by the well-oiled machine. The first was utterly useless labor. The kind of thing that, were it canceled by a simple executive order, would not alter the running of the government one iota one way or the other. The second type of work was that carried out by employees in service of their personal affairs during working hours. The third category was composed entirely of efforts to create difficulty for the general public, throwing obstacles in their path when they sought to exercise their rights. This class of work was informed by a great sense of integrity: his colleagues did everything they could to perform their duties rigorously and comprehensively. They refused absolutely everyone their rights; they stripped them of their rightful shares and kept it for the state; they stripped them of their rights and kept them for themselves. And the public came to fear these bureaucrats and to ward off their harm by means somewhat less than legal.

After that tour, Khaled kept his visits to the office down to two or three times a week. He sat, read, excused himself, left. For this, the Ministry of Foreign Affairs sent him a monthly salary. At first he didn't understand how they were calculating his compensation. Then he found out that he was paid two pounds for every paper he read within the limits of the ministry building. At this point, the thought crossed his mind that he should join one of the many civil servant syndicates and demand a raise in his wages.

For six months, he sat in his office and entertained such idle thoughts. No significant clashes occurred between him and his father during this period. After six months he entered the kitchen to get something or other, and his gaze happened to fall on a lidded basket. He paid it no heed at first. On his way out, however, he felt an urge to see what was inside the basket. He walked over and raised the lid. His blood began to boil in his veins. He heard himself saying, out loud, "The bastards!"

The basket was filled with mangoes. These had been given to his father a week ago by someone who needed his help on some matter or other. Every day some mangoes would be taken out of the basket and placed on the dining table. Anything not eaten would be placed back on the pile. This went on day after day until the pile slowly began to rot. At no point during this process had anybody considered allowing the servants to eat any of the mangoes.

The next morning, when Ahmed Pasha walked into the dining room to have his breakfast, his eyes met with a strange scene. He found his chair turned upside down. On top of this, he found a basket filled with rotten fruit. Attached to the basket was a note: "Wouldn't it have been better if the servants ate these?"

Nobody in that house could have done such a thing but Khaled.

"Did you do this?"

"Yes."

"Are you aware that the most polite word that can be used to describe this action is 'obnoxious'?"

"Mmm. And what word would you use to describe your own actions?"

Ahmed Pasha lost his temper. "Young man, I am a free man in my own house! It's time you understood that my word in this house is sacred law."

"May God Almighty forgive all of us."

"Are you mocking me?"

"You are the one who compared yourself to God."

"It appears," Ahmed Pasha said to his son, "that you consider it reasonable that someone like you criticize someone like me. Little boy, you are nothing but a simple-minded imbecile. You seem to think yourself a prodigy, the prophet of your age. In reality you are an overgrown adolescent with some deep-seated psychological issues. Your will is scattered. Your intellect is deficient. You were a sickly child, you know. Death threatened you from one moment to the next, and it affected you physically and mentally. For a while there, we thought you would be a mute, unable to put two simple words together. I only wish you could see yourself back then. You would play with the other children and you would be so much like an imbecilic monkey that they would use you as the perpetual butt of their jokes until they were fed up with you and simply tossed you to one side. Then you would hide in a corner and cry. You were a constant source of shame for me. Why don't you think about that before you open your mouth or decide on some course of action? That way you will remember who you are: a damned fool."

"Well," replied Khaled, "if foolishness is a term that can be applied to anyone who has a shameful past, then I am not the only fool."

At this point, Ahmed Pasha's Turkish roots showed themselves: rage possessed him and he screamed at his son, "What do you mean, you obnoxious dog? I have had enough of your idiocy and your ill manners. I'm warning you! One more word and I will crush you in the blink of an eye!"

Suddenly, he stopped shouting. His frown became a sly smile. He regained his sense of control and spoke in a smooth voice. "You have really disturbed me, young man, with your unique opinions. But let me ask you this: do you think you really can do real, useful work?"

The young man rallied. "I have no doubt." Then he spun around, retreated to his study, and shut the door behind him.

If he had waited just one more moment, he would have seen the smile of malicious joy on Ahmed Pasha's lips and heard him mutter, "We'll see."

# 3

MALIM WAITED A LONG TIME in the Pasha's garden. His rebellious spirit slowly returned and, though he considered simply leaving, he gathered his courage, stood up, and rang the doorbell one more time. After a moment, the Nubian servant returned, along with a scowl on his face, and asked sharply, "What do you want?"

"Have you changed your mind about fixing this window?"

"Come in."

He led Malim into the mansion, muttering to himself in his barbaric foreign tongue. Presumably, he was rounding off the insults from the previous occasion. He stopped suddenly, turned to face Malim, and asked, "Are your feet clean?"

Malim glared at him for a long moment, and then said, "No. Now show me to the broken window and stop wasting my time."

The cowardly Nubian turned away, and no sooner had he done so than he resumed his muttering, even more viciously and zealously than before. They continued to walk until they reached the room in which Khaled was resting. The Nubian knocked on the door and said, "The carpenter is here to fix the window."

"Bring him in, bring him in."

Malim asked the servant to bring him a ladder. He waited by the door, but he heard a voice calling out: "I said bring him in."

He stepped into the room nervously.

"Good morning, sir."

"Good morning!"

"If it pleases you, I'll wait outside until your servant brings me a ladder."

But Khaled just studied his face intently for a while. "What's your name?" he asked.

"Malim."

"Malim . . . Malim. I think I've seen you somewhere before."

Malim stood there, his face flushed red with embarrassment.

"Does the young bey make a habit of frequenting the neighborhood of al-Hussein?"

"Malim! Of 'a piaster for Malim' fame?"

"Yes, sir."

"But why did you leave that beautiful profession?"

"I thought I would look for an honorable one instead."

"You too, you poor bastard? Then we are colleagues. And tell me, how are you finding honorable work to be?"

"I'm working on it."

"Absurd. Isn't it? Vagrancy and idleness are more virtuous in this society of ours than work, I tell you. You couldn't even find honorable work if you tried. The only honorable thing left in this world of ours is unemployment. If your self ever whispers to you to seek any kind of work whatsoever, then it is simply leading you toward sin. You'll see, Malim. You'll see, just like I have seen."

"I'll see that actual work can't possibly be honorable?"

"Yes! Because if you seek profit from this work—which is why people look for work in the first place, you know—then you have to steal from someone. That is, if you are poor. Or you could rob the general public. Which is what I do. And what my father does. It's what anyone who owns more than one pair of shoes and one suit of clothing does, really."

"But I am doing a job, and being willingly recompensed for it. So, who am I stealing from?"

"Why, as long as society is built on a system of competition, and as long as the country is full to the brim with unemployed persons," Khaled said, "then you are stealing jobs. From other people."

The Nubian came in carrying the ladder, and Malim carried it over to the window and propped it up. He perched atop it, examining the window carefully. Khaled watched him from the other side of the room and saw a beautiful image. The light of day was coming through the fine silken curtains. It filled the room with soft light that created enchanting shadows and turned everything about them into a sort of dream. Above all this light and shadow sat Malim, cross-legged, like a prince from one of Scheherazade's stories. The young man was exceedingly beautiful, his eyes glowing with a deep and silent magic. His sharp, regular features conveyed pride and nobility. It seemed to anyone seeing him that he was descended from an ancient line of kings. All the more so because Malim did not even seem aware of his own beauty. His movements were free and natural. His voice was soft, and had about it a quality that perpetually conveyed something between apology and shyness. This young man with his humble background appeared to Khaled to be nobler than his own father, the Pasha.

Khaled did not turn his eyes away from the boy the entire time he was fixing the window, perched atop the ladder. At last, the boy moved a stray lock of hair with a toss of his head and began to descend.

"Finished?"

"No. There's something lodged in there, and it's jamming the shutters. I can't take it out unless your servant helps me pull on that cord there."

"No problem. I'll do it," said Khaled.

The shutter was the sort that could only be raised by a cord on the side of the window, and the slats would then gather in a box at the top of the window. They both worked on this mechanism for a while. Finally, Malim managed to remove the obstruction. It was a package, wrapped in paper tied by a single red ribbon.

"What is that thing, Malim?" Khaled asked.

"I don't know," Malim answered.

He leaned down from the top of the ladder and handed Khaled the package.

"Maybe it's a collection of love letters. I swear to you, if these turn out to be the old lady's I'll laugh myself to an early grave."

With that, Khaled ripped off the red ribbon and pulled open the paper packaging. But he did not find any letters, romantic or otherwise. He found it instead to be stuffed full of wads of paper currency, each note worth no less than ten pounds.

"This," he said to Malim, "is a considerable fortune."

He began to count, and soon discovered that it amounted to five hundred pounds.

He turned to Malim. "What do you think about splitting this treasure? Perhaps the old man won't come looking for it for a while. By then, the trail will have gone cold and no one will connect us to the crime."

"I'm not really in the mood for stealing right now, thanks," said Malim.

"This isn't stealing! This money is already stolen. That old man, my father, has already pillaged it from the peasants who worked so hard for it on the land he rents to them. At most, we're just sharing with him some of the money he stole. I wonder how he got all this money. How many families went hungry? How many homes were wrecked so that the Pasha could hoard some money in a box above his window . . . ? All right, Malim, don't worry. We'll give the money back to its owner. Truth is, I'm not much in the mood for theft, either."

"I'm done fixing the window."

"All right. Come back later today and I'll tell the old man to give you a reward for your trustworthiness."

"What trustworthiness? You were in the room the whole time."

"I fear," said Khaled, "that the old man will resort to just this sort of questionable logic to avoid giving you your due. He's brilliant at that sort of thing, you know. Listen up, Malim. I'll go to my room. You will wait awhile, and then call the servant and ask him to get me. Tell him you want to speak to me about something important. Now, as soon as I arrive, just hand me the package. But you have to make sure you mention nothing about the money to the servant, you understand?"

"Is it really necessary that you leave the room?" Malim asked.

"Absolutely," replied Khaled. "After all, I can't just lie and say that I left the room when I really hadn't, now could I? And in any case, you sending off for me really makes it clear how brilliantly trustworthy you are. This way, the old man will give you your fair due."

"Aren't you afraid I'll take advantage of your being gone, and just run off with the money?"

Khaled laughed. "You're not that shameless," he said. "You're poor. Maybe the likes of me would do that, if we were in your place, but not you."

Malim shrugged and said, "Listen, I really don't particularly want a reward. Don't worry about it."

"Forget all this idiotic pride. Just do what I tell you."

Khaled left the room. Malim, all alone, had no idea what to do with himself. He had to wait awhile before calling the servant, and so he walked the length of the room, pacing restlessly. His boyish impulses led him to imagine himself the master of the house, of this very room. He pretended an air of dignity and awe-inspiring respectability. He took firm, measured steps toward the desk, and began to turn over the papers on its surface as though looking for something, without ever finding his imaginary lost property. So he brought his eyebrows together, and exhaled sharply in a manner that indicated severe impatience, and then he sat at the chair in front of the desk, in deep thought. And it was while he was in this exact place that the door to the office suddenly banged open.

# 4

ON THE EVENING OF THAT same day, Malim found himself in the jailhouse appended to one of Cairo's police stations. The room was full of people of all sorts and classes. At first, they were all mixed up together, their voices all jumbled, so that anyone listening in would hear only a constant, deafening babble, rarely distinguishing one word from the next. By nightfall, however, the intensity of activity in the station eased, and the anger of the station's new guests eased with it, finally becoming completely still when they realized that all their shouting amounted to absolutely nothing.

Their jailors had stripped them of all their belongings before tossing them into the dark recesses of the room. The official excuse was that, given the mix of unsavory elements in the crowd, property had a tendency to migrate from the pockets of rightful owners to those who were possessed of somewhat more agile fingers. They were careful, however, to always leave some money in the pockets of those new residents of the jailhouse who showed signs of affluence. After all, that money would make its way naturally to the jailers in return for services rendered.

Most of the prisoners had food brought to them by their relatives. As for Malim and his ilk, who had no relatives and no friends to bring them food, they made do with the food given to them by the jail's keepers and with charity from their more well-off companions. For some time, all that could be heard was the sound of human machines consuming their fuel. Sleep was the last thing to occur for any of them. They began to split into separate groups, each group killing time with their late-night conversations and, eventually, something akin to joy began to spread among this gathering of outlaws. As night had first fallen, there could be heard, here and there, the sounds of weeping and wailing, but now, in the depths of the night, there was only the sound of laughter to be heard in that dark room with its revolting odors.

The loudest group was composed of a number of students who were arrested during a demonstration. But the laughter of this group was not the result of genuine mirth. They were afraid. Their chests were tight with fear. But they were too proud to show it in front of this crowd. After all, they were the vanguard of sound opinion, the intellectual leaders of the people. And that was why their voices were louder than anybody else's, even though the quaking of their hearts was mightier.

The truth was that there appeared on the faces of these students none of the signs of courage, and it could perhaps be said that such demonstrations were, for them, less a form of revolution than a sort of break from homework. The whole thing was nothing more than a few lone individuals shouting some slogans that were in turn repeated by others. One of them points at a road, and the crowd of students pushes forward in that direction, yelling and wailing. A street lamp might get in their way. They smash its glass casing. Or perhaps it's a tree. They uproot it. People come out onto their balconies to watch and be entertained. If the crowd of students passes a balcony with some pretty girls, the demonstration pauses for a second underneath that balcony, and the revolutionary cries get even louder for a moment, and gestures and greetings proliferate all of a sudden. Arguments break out under the balcony. Some of the demonstrators want to have a whole other kind of demonstration. But then the tram passes by, and the demonstrators attack it, crowding it from all sides. Finally, the police arrive, and they arrest a young man here, and a young man there. In the blink of an eye, the demonstration is no more.

Besides these students there were two other groups in the jail with Malim. The first of these was the group making the least noise, though it was also the group that did the most talking. Its members were the least remarkable of the people in the jail. They were not members of the middle class, but they could not be counted among the poor masses either. They were in many ways related to both classes at once. Some of them dressed in Western clothing, some dressed in rural clothing, and some mixed both styles. They were a mix of minor merchants, drivers, and owners of small street cafés. They adopted an artificial air of respectability designed to make the others feel that they were not like them. It was just a mistake—an insignificant mistake—that had led them to this place. As soon as dawn broke this mistake would be uncovered and they would be released, their dignity intact. The only subject of conversation among them was the nature of that insignificant mistake. Each of them explained in detail the series of strange coincidences that had led to the accusations against him, and clarified precisely the incontrovertible evidence that proved his innocence. These were the ones who had never ever done any wrong whatsoever, and who made up the overwhelming majority of the citizens of the world.

As for the last group, they were those in whose lives jail was not really considered a critical event. After all, there is no profession that is completely free of hardship, and jail was just one of the nuisances of their chosen profession. This group was distinguished by the fact that its members never stopped laughing. They mocked themselves and others. They mocked the rulers. They mocked the ruled. Life was an amusing anecdote to them, and any subject they discussed was colored by this attitude. There was among them a young man with a melodious voice, and they insisted that he sing for them. He sang a lament about the vicissitudes of time. Miserable, overpowering time.

Malim could never be sure afterward why his eyes had flooded with tears when he heard that song echo in the dark grave of a room that contained the dregs of humanity. Before that song, he was in full control of himself. None of it

44

bothered him, except the overwhelming heat and the disgusting, unbearable odor. But he felt no fear. In fact, he had felt a kind of relief when the journey had ended in this stone space, cursed by God and man. At least the damned day was over, and with it the torture he had experienced at the hands of those cruel policemen. He could rest now, for a moment, from their threats. For a while, he would not have to hear the insults, thrown at him from every mouth. He wouldn't have to look at the faces of those human wolves that had thrown him in this jail, instead of giving him the reward they had promised. Was this really the recompense of that honorable work for the sake of which he had rejected his first life?

Malim saw all kinds of scum in that prison. He watched fathers condemn their sons to escape punishment, and thieves sell each other out. He saw friends betray friends. Women who had spent their husbands' money on their lovers, and denied that same money to their own children. Husbands who forced their women to work jobs honorable and dishonorable while they themselves did nothing but spend the money they made. But of all the scum that passed his gaze, he saw no bastard more despicable than Omar, who was Khaled's older brother. The rest of them were forced into contemptible behavior by necessity. But this particular lowlife sought out contemptible behavior for the sheer pleasure of it.

He would never forget the words that bastard said in front of the investigator. It seemed they were waiting for the arresting policemen to bring Malim to them, because the investigator did not take Omar's testimony until after Malim arrived. Malim found them gathered together in the study where he had been fixing their window. Among them was an old man with a scowling face, who shot daggers at him, and bellowed, "Is this the swine?"

"That's the one, Father," Omar answered.

Khaled, in the meantime, was sitting in the corner of the room. He did not say a word.

Omar began to give his report to the investigator. "I came back from the ministry a little earlier than usual. I had very important papers with me for some work I had to complete that evening. Which is why I passed by the study to place those papers there before going to my room. When I opened the door I found this boy trying to break into the drawer."

Malim could not bear the lie, and shouted, "That's not true!"

But the policeman unleashed a torrent of abuse toward him. "Shut your mouth, you bastard! Were you not sitting at the desk?"

"Yes."

"You were writing a letter, I suppose? Or perhaps you were reading a novel."

Malim did not answer him, because he didn't know what to say.

"If you open your mouth one more time, dog, you can be sure I have ways to shut you up. Sergeant, get him acquainted with how we silence noisy animals," the officer said. Whereupon the sergeant struck Malim a blow that almost knocked him unconscious.

"Please, Omar Bey," the officer continued, "did the accused have any tools with him?"

"Oh, yes, he did. Many tools. They were on the desk. He hadn't yet started to use them."

Khaled broke his silence for the first time. "Those are the tools of his trade, officer. Of course he had them with him!"

Ahmed Pasha stiffened, and sparks shot from his eyes. "Khaled! Have some respect for the due process of the law! When I was a prosecutor I would never allow someone to interrupt a witness. If it were done twice I would remove him from the room. Please do not force this officer to do the same to you."

"When the boy saw me he was visibly shaken," Omar continued. "He seemed at a loss for what to do. I asked him what he was doing there, and he answered me, stuttering and stammering, that he was there to fix the window. I called the servant, who confirmed this fact. I then went to the desk and checked its drawers and found them intact, and glanced at the room and found nothing missing. So I let the boy go and rebuked the servant for leaving him alone in the room. He responded that Khaled had been watching the boy and did not call the servant back in when he left. When my father came home, I told him the story and he told me where he had left five hundred pounds when he lost the keys to his safe. I ordered the servant to bring me a ladder and went myself to the window to retrieve the money, but found no trace of it. At that point my father had no choice but to call the police."

It was on the basis of this testimony that Malim was charged. And then it was Khaled's turn to bear witness. But Khaled was confused. He didn't quite know what to say. At first he thought some error would make itself known naturally and demonstrate Malim's innocence. Perhaps the boy had found some difficulty in calling for Khaled in the manner they had agreed upon. Or perhaps his avidness for the reward, his desire to give the money to the Pasha himself, caused him to hesitate to give the money to Omar. Oh, how he wished he could have spoken to Malim in private, before the investigator arrived. If he knew what the circumstances were, he could tailor his testimony to help Malim. But his father had called the police immediately, and he only saw the boy when the police brought him in after he was already under arrest.

At first, Khaled leaned toward leaving out the conspiracy he and Malim had cooked up. It followed from this that he would deny seeing any money with Malim in the first place. His pride simply could not take standing there before his father as a thief who had conspired to relieve him of a paltry sum of money. But when he heard his brother's testimony, he realized that the accusation against Malim had almost been established as fact. And in any case, Malim would no doubt mention the whole thing when he was called upon to give his account. It was only wise, then, to tell the story now, since that would strengthen the boy's position.

At the same time, he was disturbed by another thought. What if the boy said that he had in fact already given Khaled the money before he left the room? His story of the deal between him and Malim would then sound incredible. He could picture now how the investigator would smile when he heard it. It would sound like any of the dozens of ridiculous stories he heard every day from petty criminals who wished to cover up their crimes.

The officer asked him to declare his name, age, and place of residence. Then he asked, "What do you know of this incident, Khaled Bey?"

Khaled began to recount the details of the incident. When he reached the point where Malim found the money, he hesitated. A moment later he heard himself recounting the story, though he had not intended to.

"And did he then give you the money?"

"Yes."

The Pasha stirred in his seat, and then said in a voice seething with rage, "You did not mention this to me when I asked you."

"Well, that's what happened."

The investigator interrupted, "And then what happened, Khaled Bey?"

The moment of truth had arrived. There was no way out now: he simply had to tell them the whole conspiracy in all its sordid details. How desperate Khaled was at this point! He could see his father's frown deepening and deepening as he told the story. He could see the marks of surprise on the face of the officer, and it seemed to him that he could also see the beginnings of that damnable smile, just as he had expected. It almost drove Khaled mad. He was now the prime suspect in the eyes of the investigator: first he said he took the money, then he said he left the room. What sane person would believe that he gave such a sum back to Malim before leaving? How stupid he was, and how foolish.

He felt actual gratitude toward his father when he heard him say, "I hope, officer, that you do not believe a single word this young man is saying."

Then he turned to Khaled, yelling, "Are you not ashamed of yourself? This is not the time for these deranged fantasies of yours. Not to mention that you are wasting this officer's time."

He turned to the officer once more. "Sir, this young man is famously eccentric. I have suffered much from him, and experience has shown me that not everything he says is exactly the truth. He has some perverse and immature tendencies that sometimes drive him to say things he thinks are true, even if they are completely misguided. He seems to think that he can get this boy off the hook, and he is willing to say whatever it takes to do that."

"Don't worry about it, Your Excellency," said the officer, who was highly amused. "The truth will make itself known in the end." And then he turned to Malim and asked, "Is what Khaled Bey said true?"

"Yes," Malim answered curtly.

The Pasha, unable to contain himself, objected. "You shouldn't have asked that, officer!"

The officer did not want someone questioning the way he did his job, and certainly not in front of his subordinates. He in turn could not contain his response. "I think it would be best if His Excellency the Pasha would just let me conduct my own investigation."

"Oh, absolutely," the Pasha retorted. "That is not a right with which I would ever allow myself to interfere. But I ask you: what exactly were you expecting the boy to say? He is fighting for his very survival, and here is a unique opportunity to escape, so how could he not seize it? Remember that I am older than you, son. I have investigated crimes for many a year, and I hope you will take my counsel. The best way to conduct an investigation is to have a complete theory about what in fact happened. Questions should be designed to confirm that theory. Otherwise one sees nothing but mystery and confusion. The defense will find many holes to take advantage of, and often criminals go free who are clearly guilty. And all this could have been avoided had the persecuting party presented a watertight case, solid and without chinks."

Khaled heard this theory and recognized it as the perfect expression of his father's black soul, and his constant urge to harm his fellow man. He almost cried out against the corruption of this theory, but he held his silence. He had shown enough stupidity and foolishness, and the result had been catastrophe. Perhaps he would be silent for once and perhaps also his father's expounding on his opinions would be what saved them from this crisis.

As for the officer, he simply repeated what he had said before: "Don't worry, Your Excellency, the truth will make itself known in the end."

And the Pasha thought, How stupid you are!

The officer turned back to Khaled. "And then, Khaled Bey? Did the boy call for you as you agreed he should?"

"No."

"What happened?"

"I don't know. I did not see the boy again until he arrived here just a few moments ago."

"And were you confident that the boy would follow through with your plan?"

And here, Khaled saw a gleam of hope. If he took advantage of this opportunity intelligently, he could escape this predicament in which he had found himself. He was thinking only of himself now. And if he hesitated for a second, it was only to perfect the plan that he had determined to carry out.

"The truth is that I felt at the time that I could trust him. But now that I think about it, it seems I may have been wrong."

"Did he do something that suggested that he was untrustworthy, then?"

"Yes. Before I left the room, he said, 'Aren't you afraid that I will take advantage of your being gone, and just run off with the money?' And since he did not return the money, it is possible that the idea grew on him when he found himself alone and free to do what he wanted."

Anger grew in Malim. He couldn't stop himself from objecting: "Now you?"

But the officer cut him off sharply. "Watch your manners, boy! Did you say those words to Khaled Bey?"

"Yes. Yes, I did. But this bey knows full well that I said it to him jokingly."

The officer laughed mockingly. "It's always easy for a criminal to say 'I was joking.'"

But Malim too laughed mockingly. "It's only the jokes of the poor that aren't believable," he said.

"What is that supposed to mean?"

Malim looked at Khaled. "He knows exactly what I mean," he said. "He can tell you if he wishes."

"Never mind him, Khaled Bey. Do you have anything else you'd like to add?"

Khaled's face looked like that of a corpse. "This boy, raised in alleyways and among the rabble, how could he be so much nobler of character than me?" Khaled thought to himself.

His heart beat against his chest. The world felt like it was slipping away from him. What is wrong with me? he wondered. How could he allow himself to sink to this level, to be this contemptible, to not care about the consequences that would be suffered by this poor wretch?

The silence grew.

"Do you have anything to add, Khaled Bey?"

Khaled startled, and answered with a voice that seemed to come from the hollow of the grave. "What? No. No."

It was now Malim's turn to give his account, and it was the same as Khaled's down to the smallest detail. When he reached the point where Khaled left the room, he said, "After a minute or two, the door opened and Omar Bey came in. And it's true. I was sitting at the desk. But I was not playing with the drawer like he said. And the tools were not on the desk, they were by the door. When he asked me what I was doing, I told him I would like to speak to Khaled Bey about a private matter. He reprimanded me, and was surprised that I could have some sort of private affair with his brother. He said that I could certainly tell him something I could tell his own sibling. I became very embarrassed, because he was right. But I couldn't tell him about the plan Khaled Bey had come up with. So all I could do was tell him that I found the money and where I had found it."

"And then what happened?"

"I gave him the money."

Omar jumped from his chair, yelling, "Liar! Barefaced liar!"

Malim looked at him calmly for a long moment. "I am not a liar. And you know very well that I am not a thief."

The officer laughed out loud. "The fact is, Your Excellency" he said, "that I have never seen a criminal this bold."

He turned to Malim and asked, "So you are accusing Omar Bey of stealing the money?"

"I'm not accusing anyone of anything. I'm saying I gave him the money. But I don't know what he did with it."

"Excellent, excellent. And then?"

"And then, Omar Bey stood a long time thinking. After a while, I saw him ringing the bell for the servant, who came and was asked why I was in the room alone, and then yelled at me harshly. I couldn't stand seeing this from someone who had the actual proof I was innocent in his own pocket. I objected, but he shut me up violently, and ordered the servant to throw me out into the street. And then a bit later, these two cops came and arrested me and here I am."

These memories overwhelmed Malim as he sat on the floor of the jail, and then he fell asleep.

# 5

KHALED GENTLY PUSHED OPEN THE door to his brother's room. He stood for a moment, listening. When he was sure no one was in there, he shut the door carefully and advanced slowly, on the tips of his toes. Somewhere in the middle of the room he was startled by his reflection in a mirror and stopped suddenly.

For a moment he felt hysterical laughter welling up in him. His reflection reminded him of those Arsène Lupin novels. All he needed now was a small pistol in one hand and a small dagger in the other.

But he had no time for laughter or ironic thoughts about detective novels. He had a mission, and he had to complete it as soon as possible, before someone saw him in his brother's room. If he could find some material evidence, then he could free Malim. As for the circumstantial evidence, fate had provided it only an hour ago.

Khaled was in his room at the time, reading a book that had arrived in the mail that very morning. He was completely engrossed, devouring it voraciously, when the phone rang. It kept ringing and ringing, and nobody paid it any heed. It seemed there was no way to stop it but to go and pick it up himself.

"Hello. Who is this?"

A somewhat disreputable female voice asked, "Omar?"

This was not the first time an incident like this had occurred. Quite often, in fact, he would pick up the phone and various female voices would make the same inquiry of him: "Omar?" The reason for this was the fact that, despite the sharp contrasts between him and his brother, their voices were identical. So much so that with closed eyes one simply could not tell which of them was speaking. Whenever one of these women asked him that traditional question—"Omar?"— he would yell at them. He would tell them that time was a valuable commodity, and then he would lament the corrupt society that had made all women into mere harlots, chasing after men. Usually, before he reached the point in the sermon where he gave the good news that one day women would truly be independent and free, and no longer in need of this sort of artificiality, etcetera, the particular woman at hand would have ended the conversation with a flood of derision, and topped it off with a mocking laugh, or perhaps with some gentle advice to relax and get a grip.

This time, however, he was curious to see what this woman had to say to his brother. He did not take his usual approach but simply said that, yes, he was indeed Omar. The woman asked him about one thing after another, and he answered her vaguely, which in turn led her to ask him why he was not his usual playful self. Perhaps, she suggested, he was angry with her? Khaled denied this enthusiastically. "I'm just feeling a bit under the weather today."

"Oh, darling, I do hope you get better soon. But please tell me you aren't mad at me. I know I've been awfully rude for not thanking you for that astonishing gift. But let me explain. When you sent that necklace the other day I could not believe those were real diamonds. Today I went over to the jeweler and he assured me that every single stone was real, and offered to buy it for four hundred pounds! I told him I would never give this gift up, even if he offered me ten times that amount. From that moment I knew beyond any doubt that my dear Omar really and truly loved me, the way I love him. Suad, your faithful girl, is simply dying to see you. I want to show you just how grateful I am. Tell me, are you coming tonight?"

"Where?

"What kind of question is that? To the usual place."

"Oh, I heard some rumors that you had signed up with another place."

"Oh, will people never stop with these rumors? Don't worry about that—I am still at Samiha's place."

"Very well then, my dear, sweet, lovely Suad. Au revoir."

So there it was. Malim was the most honest man among them. After all, where would Omar get four hundred pounds, when he had borrowed five pounds from Khaled himself less than a week ago? He knew his brother was a philanderer. He specialized in women the way some scientists specialized in one particular species of bacteria. He was reckless and a spendthrift, and, despite the fact that he possessed a graduate degree, he was a functional illiterate, whose only literary output was the papers he had to sign at the same ministry that the Pasha had forced on Khaled to keep him as far away as possible from reading and writing. Omar's life was the life of Omar al-Khayyam. Save that he had substituted Khayyam's obsession with bodies of water for an obsession with some cabarets. He was also a liar, skilled in hypocrisy, and had mastered the trick of charming deception. This last characteristic was the secret of his closeness to their father. For, despite the fact that Ahmed Pasha was well aware of his son's deceptions, he always seemed perfectly willing to forgive them. The issue with Ahmed Pasha, as it was with most people, was one of interactions and not simply of actions. And Omar interacted with his father in a way that charmed him and secured his approval. A wise son knows his father's weak points and uses them to get close to him. It was always "Baba Pasha," and standing up when he entered the room, and not sitting until permission was granted. He did not speak until spoken to, and always answered questions in a tremulous voice that betrayed awe and respect. He had never once forgotten to kiss his father's hand in the morning.

Khaled knew all this about his brother. But he did not know that he was capable of stealing. Or that he could allow himself to destroy the life of a poor boy. And here he was doing both at once.

Khaled, the private detective, did not really have his work cut out. He knew that his brother left all his drawers open except one, which he locked and kept the key with him at all times. This was the drawer where he kept all the letters and little souvenirs from his various lovers. How often had he shown Khaled this merchandise and forced upon him the stories that related to them? He called it the Drawer of Desire.

What Khaled was looking for was in the Drawer of Desire. Opening the Drawer of Desire was the easiest thing in the world. All he had to do was remove the drawer above it and reach through the opening that made, and everything in the Drawer of Desire would be his.

On the evening of that same day, Khaled knocked on the door of his father's room, saying, "Father, I have come seeking Ahmed Pasha, the man of justice."

Ahmed Pasha looked at his son suspiciously, then said, "Just come out and say it."

Khaled took out a red band and showed it to his father. "Do you remember this?"

The Pasha took it with some surprise and stared at it for a while. He did not answer.

"And do you remember this?" Khaled showed him an envelope printed with the legend "National Bank of Egypt."

The Pasha snatched them both from Khaled's hand, and said darkly, "Where did you find these?"

"In Omar's room."

"And how am I to believe that? I have no trust left in you."

"He still has fifty pounds in his drawer, and they are crisp, untouched, still in the wrapping the bank put them in."

"How do you know that?"

"I've seen it with my own eyes. I can show you if you like."

"So! You have permitted yourself to snoop around your brother's room in his absence!"

"Yes. I was unjust to Malim, and sometimes two wrongs make a right."

"And where is the rest of the money?"

"He bought a necklace with it. For a belly dancer at Samiha's Dance Hall. I can prove every word of what I am telling you."

Ahmed Pasha collapsed into his chair and rested his head on his hands. For a long moment he stayed there, and then he muttered, "Steal from me! From his own father, the source of his success?"

Khaled almost smiled, almost said, "Like father, like son." But he did not smile, and he did not say anything. He contented himself with looking for a moment at his father's bald spot. After a while, Ahmed Pasha raised his head and gave his son a challenging glare, asking, "And you? What do you want?"

"What I want is clear, Father."

"I suppose you want me to force Omar to confess his crime?"

"You of all people should know that the law is not as strict on sons who steal from their fathers. No harm will come to Omar if he confesses."

"And in the interest of what exactly do you want me to dishonor my family name in this terrible way?"

"In the interest of justice for poor Malim."

"Malim. Are you serious? Who is this Malim? I would spend a thousand Malims for the sake of maintaining the reputation of one Khorshed."

"The overseer of your estate said those very same words when Omar wanted to get his hands on his daughter. He said that he would kill a thousand Khorsheds before letting a single one of them touch a hair on his daughter's head. These are lovely phrases. Very inspiring. But they have no meaning."

"How stupid you are! The thin shell on the surface of your mind, which you think is intelligence, is nothing but a fragile cover for a deep stupidity. Society, boy, is not a simple collection of individuals. It is composed of families. Great families. And these families sacrifice other souls in order to survive and to maintain their reputations. You come to speak to me as a just judge. Well, as a judge, I see that true justice—not the appearance of justice, but true justice—is the justice that fosters the security of society and its progress. And that justice necessitates the sacrifice of Malim for the purpose of maintaining a great family like mine."

"We have a name for that kind of thinking, you know," Khaled said. "We call it feudalism. That time has passed, and we are now in another time: the time of freedom and equality. And something else. Why do you call our family great? If it is a matter of numbers, well, the family of your chauffeur is greater. And as for lineage, neither of us knows our ancestors beyond the third generation. We don't even know who started this family. It was probably some wretch selling basterma from a cart. And yet there are peasant families who can trace their lineage back seven generations. We're not a big family, and we're not a family with lineage, and this is not the age of feudalism. So let's just try and save Malim."

Khaled said these things without fully being aware of what he was saying. When he regained his awareness, he was sorry that he had said what he said, for he needed his father's good pleasure, and he assumed that his father would be angered by his words. And that was why he was surprised when he saw that old abhorrent smile on his father's face. "Very well, you glorious hero, son of the seller of basterma. I will work toward saving Malim. On one condition."

"And that is?"

"That you give me back my money."

"That's a conversation you should have with Omar."

"But you were kind enough to inform me that Omar spent the money he took. How can he give that money back?"

"And who do you think is going to give it back to you? Malim?"

"Oh, yes, boy. Yes. That workshop that Malim is apprenticed in belongs to a very prominent contractor. If Malim is found guilty, well, then I am entitled by law to demand my money back from that contractor."

Now that they were talking money, Khaled thought, reason was not going to do the job. He thought he would try to appeal to his father's emotions. "Do you not feel a deep pain in your heart, Father, when you sit in your quiet sitting room in the evenings and recall that you are the reason some poor boy has been pulled out of his world and dragged into a dark, dirty cell?"

"Do you think this boy of yours lived at the Continental? I have done this boy a favor. He's in a cleaner place now than where he used to live. He's eating better food. I guarantee you, for that type, prison is a blessing, not a punishment."

So much for pathos. All that was left was threats.

"So you will not change your mind?"

"Just like you won't change your mind."

"Then you are forcing me to become your adversary in a court of law. I will testify before a judge about everything I said here today."

"It won't help you one little bit. You have no proof."

"Let's say I could prove that Omar spent an amount similar to the stolen amount and around the same time?"

"Then I will testify that I loaned him that amount, and that it is not the money I am missing."

"And the envelope from the bank?"

"You won't have it," he said, as he slipped it into the inside pocket of his jacket.

Rage rose up in Khaled. He felt himself moving toward his father. His hands became fists.

The Pasha retreated, trembling and shouting, "Get out! Out, you criminal!"

But Khaled continued to move slowly toward him. "I am not leaving without that envelope."

The Pasha was now hiding behind his desk. He was frantically ringing a bell and screaming. "You are trying to kill me, you little bastard. Saleh! Omar! Come and restrain this criminal."

The door swung open and Saleh, the Nubian servant, ran in. Ahmed Pasha collapsed into his chair, panting with terror.

"Stop him, Saleh! He wants to kill me. Hold his arms! Get him out of here!"

Khaled found himself in the strong arms of the Nubian. Now that he felt safe, the Pasha became once more a proud lion, standing tall and haughty with his nose in the air. He declared grandly, "You will not spend the night under my roof!"

Khaled answered him with fire in his eyes, "Not this night, not any other night. This is goodbye. Forever."


The sentence in Malim's case was set at three years with hard labor. Throughout the trial, which took three sessions to conclude, he remained completely silent. When asked to give his testimony, he did not open his mouth. The prosecution and the defense both asked him questions, and he did not utter a single word. The judge was furious. He screamed and threatened.

Malim stared steadily at the iron bars and it was as if he hadn't heard any of the demands to speak his part. Khaled asked him what was the matter and begged him to speak. Malim's only response was to smile and shrug. He was like a nobleman who found himself the prisoner of some barbaric tribesmen. He was utterly unconcerned about establishing his innocence according to their standards. The rituals performed by their sorcerers and priests were mere performances by which they satisfied their own impulses and humiliated their prisoner. But of course, the prisoner would meet the same fate even were he to fill the horizon with screams and appeals for mercy. It was far more dignified to maintain one's silence.

As for Khaled, his was an entirely different attitude. Good intentions joined forces with inexperience and the recklessness of youth. He was the perfect example of the ignorant friend. That is, he was more harmful than a sane enemy. His testimony in front of the judge was not that of an impartial witness, but of a defending attorney deducing from the evidence. He was plainly presenting a certain reality, marshaling the forces of logic to prove the innocence of the accused. And so his testimony rang false. Ahmed Pasha's attorney did not, of course, miss this opportunity. He stung Khaled with his sarcasm and the courtroom rang with laughter. Nor did it end there. The strange stories Khaled told, the detective novel–inspired nature of his actions, all of this led the judge to be somewhat suspicious of Khaled's testimony. Moreover, he quickly grew irate with the confused imaginings that he viewed as wasting the court's precious time, not to mention the contempt he felt for this wayward son who would abuse his father in this way. And of course, his father was a great man, feared by the community. This all showed: he interrupted Khaled harshly, declared his opinions foolish, mocked him, and violently rebuffed him whenever he wished to comment on a particular incident or mentioned his father. He finally declared publicly his sadness at this conduct by a son toward his father.

No wonder then that Khaled's eyes were filled with tears when he had completed his testimony. He was in a state that evoked pity in people of kind hearts and mirth in the rest. If Ahmed Pasha had been there, he would not have been able to contain his joy.

Ahmed Pasha's attorney was a giant in his field. He was extremely influential and had a grand reputation. His mere presence in a courtroom was enough, sometimes, to change the appearance of the truth. Also, because he had been an attorney for a long time, he knew that judges, when faced with details, had a tendency to fall asleep. And so he approached the accusation in a general sort of way. He focused his attack on one weak spot, so his proofs lined up perfectly and his words were strung together like measured pearls. In this way, the truth took the shape he crafted, took the path he laid out for it. When he was done, the ears of the audience members simply would not accept an image of the events other than that which he fashioned with his silver tongue and his evocative, seductive allusions.

As for Malim's lawyer, he was a young man, a friend of Khaled's. So no wonder that his defense met with the same fate as Khaled's testimony. He thought that the older attorney did not speak much because he was not cognizant of all the details, and because he did not understand the case. As for himself, well, he had read the entire file ten times over. He was all: "Firstly . . . and secondly . . . and thirdly . . ." until the audience was bored, and, feeling that boredom, the young lawyer stuttered, and, stuttering, he lost his composure. His loss of composure led him to lose the thread of the argument he had painstakingly prepared. He felt suspended somewhere between heaven and earth. He was muttering unconnected words, leading nowhere in particular. He would pause for a moment and then say, "And additionally . . ." but then would not add anything. He would fiddle with his papers, but they seemed to reveal nothing to him. Things reached a crisis point. He said things that were not in fact in the interest of the defendant and confused the public prosecutor. His colleagues alerted him to his errors, or laughed at him. The judge asked him regularly, "Sir, are you done?"

It had to end as soon as possible, of course. And so the young attorney declared in conclusion that, "Based on all this, my good sirs, it is clear that the defendant is guilty beyond all doubt." And the courtroom shook with the laughter of all present.

And in this way, between the ill intentions of the father and the good intentions of the son, Malim lost a year and a half of his life.

# 6

IT WAS A HABIT WITH Khaled to insist, every now and then, that he hated literature and anything that smacked of fiction. That he did not understand, for example, why anyone would ever read a novel. At best, novels were an inaccurate representation of reality. And in any case, reality was evident. He could see it for himself and had no need to read about it in a book. He could experience it directly, and did not require a middleman.

He would boast that he had never been caught red-handed with a novel in his life. He could exaggerate, saying that he would not even read a book where he himself was the protagonist, even if it were written by a great novelist. This could be understood as a natural extension of his opinion that novels were useless. But a psychoanalyst might suggest that the reason was more significant. He might suggest that there were parts of Khaled's life of which he was ashamed, and that his shame would be greater were it to be placed before the gaze of a novelist, since this would reveal things a more casual eye might have missed.

Perhaps the most shameful of these moments was that night when he left his father's house with the intention never to return.

That night, Khaled went to a friend's house on the outskirts of Cairo. He spent the whole night thinking about what he would do the next day, and the day after that. He would leave the job his father had found him—that was certain. The question, put simply, was: how was he to make a living? He couldn't do one of those serious jobs that actually put food on the table—that was also certain. He could no longer be an employee without an occupation. He could neither do what he had done, nor could he do any other work, since any work that involved earning one's daily bread was mechanical and petty. It was thoughtless work. It could do irreparable damage to his spiritual development. As for the life of being a thinker, that was certain to make its adherents homeless and hungry, and inspired nothing but contempt from one's peers. The status of an artist or a writer in a country like Egypt, which had only a modest claim to civilization at best, was somewhere between a truck driver and a court clerk.

He wrestled with these thoughts until a beautiful pink sunrise broke on the horizon. But looking at it from the balcony, it seemed to Khaled like an eye bloodshot from weeping. He had glanced at his own eyes when he left, and it seemed to him as though this sunrise were nothing but the reflection of his own state in the mirror of nature.

Since his friend's home was built on the edge of the desert that surrounded Cairo, he saw in this desert a few huts belonging to some Bedouin Arabs, and in front of them was a stretch of land with some herbage where a few skinny goats were grazing. Some tribesmen were lighting a fire nearby. Suddenly, Khaled was inspired. Or you could say that he received a revelation. He was an Arab. And he would share with them the life of a nomadic Arab. How joyful the life of a Bedouin is, filled as it is with sword duels and bullets. Was he not a knight, as capable of fighting as they were? It was no coincidence that he had been a fencing champion at the English college where he studied. He was a horseman too, and had once taken a horse on a long trip in the desert of Siwa and enjoyed himself very much. All these were well-known signs that he was possessed of a sound Arab nature, although the corruption of the society he lived in had blinded him to that fact until this very moment.

Two days later, a couple of Bedouin were building him a hut out of reeds nearby. On the third day, Khaled spent his first night there. In a week, there was a young Arab in Bedouin robe and headdress living there, and his name was Khaled. Yes, this young man, who had always lamented the romanticism of his fellow man, was himself, it seemed, vulnerable to being the ultimate romantic.

His friend came in one morning and Khaled insisted on lighting a fire and making him a cup of tea in the Arab tradition. His friend made a futile attempt to argue that the house was a stone's throw away and that they could just bring tea from there. But where would be the Arab chivalry in that? What would Hatem, the generous hero of Arab history, do when he heard such a thing?

"How could you come to my home, as my guest, and yet be the one to provide for me?"

His friend laughed and said nothing more. After a heroic effort, Khaled presented him with the tea in a clay cup. It was terrible. No sooner had he taken his first sip than Khaled asked, "How do you find it?"

"The tea?"

"Yes."

"Hot."

"This is desert tea. You won't exactly find it like this in Café Groppi, you know."

His friend laughed. "Sure. You won't find anything like this anywhere."

"What's that supposed to mean?" Khaled said defensively.

"Nothing."

"Why are you laughing?"

"No reason. No reason at all."

Khaled jumped to his feet, shouting, "You are mocking me!"

"Sit down, Bedouin!"

"Why are you laughing?"

"I just thought about something funny. You remember when we were in England, we had friends who were materialists? They sometimes saw traditional ways as primitive superstition, or viewed them as the wild imaginings of poets with weak digestion."

"And?"

"I've met some people here in Egypt who are like this."

"And?"

"And I noticed a strange thing. I noticed that those who have the imaginations of poets are really, in their behavior, the most pragmatic of people. Materialistic even, quite often. So we say, well, those are the weak of faith. But you, you're even stranger. All you believe in are algebraic formulas, but your actions remind me of the actions of an eighteenth-century Romantic. You remind me of Byron actually. Or maybe Shelley, I don't know. I know another algebraic guy of your type who lives in total solitude and does nothing but listen to music, as if he's a monk, worshiping. What is there to say about people like you who can't seem to stay away from the very flaws your beliefs warn you against?"

"Perhaps we're weak in our madness too."

Khaled wore his Bedouin garb for two weeks—although his official account is three weeks. During that time, he bought a goat, which he milked every morning. But he felt that the image was still not complete. So he bought a loom and some wool, and he began to weave. He would socialize with his Bedouin neighbors and sit with them. He came back one day and threw away his shaving equipment. After a while he saw that his growing beard, when combined with his glasses, made him look more like a Jewish moneylender than a heroic Arab. So he threw away his glasses.

And so on.

Then one night, he crossed the few meters that separated him from his friend's house and knocked on the door because he was reading a book and there was no light in his hut. In fact, the books he wanted to finish had piled up because of the lack of lighting. Also, his cunning friend had remarked, "It's so hot these days. Doesn't all this clothing bother you?"

"Yes."

The next day Khaled was wearing shorts and an open shirt. Then he started not spending the night in the hut. In a few days he was not eating his meals there either. Then his friend's birthday came around, and Khaled insisted on slaughtering the goat for him. When it grew even hotter, it became quite unbearable to spend the daytime hours in the hut, so he went there only in the evenings.

And so on.

The hut was abandoned after a little more than a month, although Khaled insisted that it was two months. His cunning friend now said to him, "Do you think it would be a good idea to knock that hut down?"

Khaled stared at his friend's shapely young maid, who was serving the food, and said, "Maybe I'll spend the night there sometimes."

The maid blushed and lowered her gaze.

One day, a messenger came and said his mother's illness had reached a crisis point, and that she wanted to see him. He hurried to her, and when she saw him she reached her hand out to him, and he bent over it to kiss it, speechless, words stuck in his throat. He looked at his mother's face and saw the young twenty-year-old woman she had been. He felt a vast love for her filling him, but he didn't know how to express it without weeping. His mother on her deathbed was not that interminably tedious woman. That woman who, in her loneliness, was forced to entertain herself by creating insincere habits that disgusted him. She was now just a kind human being, naive, like an infant just out of its mother's womb.

How painful this moment was for his conscience. The truth was that his mother had always been this kind, naive human being. But he had never made the effort to crack that thin external shell and penetrate to her beautiful interior. He was selfish. He criticized people, but did not bother to see the beautiful side of them. She must have been very hurt by the way he treated her. He was polite to her, but did not give her the affection that sustained her, that she needed so much. Yes, his mother's state would have been very different if she had simply been shown some affection by her husband or her children. But the whole family had turned away from her, and had she not been a wealthy woman she would have been in a truly miserable state.

How he wished, as he held her hand, that he could turn back the clock. That he could sit by her side in the evenings until she was in the embrace of sleep. That he could wake her with kisses as though he were her husband. If he could only go back and seek her, divulge to her all his affairs, make her his partner in all his joys and sorrows. He wished he could take her as a mother, a sister, a friend.

But she was dying.

He didn't return to his friend's house that evening. He spent the night at the hut. His mother had died in his arms. The look of love and gratitude she had given him had not left him for even a second since then. She had given him that look to show him that she had forgiven him. But forgiveness was conclusive proof of guilt.

It dawned on him that he had killed his mother. For if he had only loved her, she would not have died. If he had not left home, she would not have died.

After a month of this, his father said to him, "You have killed your mother. Your hands are covered in her blood."

Ahmed Pasha threw this accusation at his son at the end of a long, brutal argument that lasted an endless hour. It was as if the man could read his mind. But Khaled regained some control over himself, conjured an ironic smile, and said simply, "Like father, like son."

"If you are going to be like that again, then we should just end this conversation."

"We should have ended it long ago. I don't even know why you insisted on my coming here. The minute I arrived you began smooth-talking me, and I'm not sure why. All I know is that, for some reason, you want my good will. Suddenly you want to give me a monthly allowance, to spend however I want. All of a sudden, you want me back in your house. So just tell me: what do you want?"

Ahmed Pasha rose from his chair, nose high in the air. "Young man," he said, "your ill manners have grown beyond all limits. I see that I am forced to ask you once more to leave my house."

"And I see that I am forced to remind you once more that I am in the house of my dear departed mother, and that it is possible that I have inherited more of it than you have."

"It saddens me to tell you, my young effendi, that you have inherited nothing from your mother."

"Oh? Why is that? Has it finally been revealed that I am not my mother's son?"

"Your dear departed mother sold me this house and everything else she owned in return for debts that she owed me."

"Debts. Why? Did you practice usury with her?"

"That's not your concern."

"Whose concern is it, then? My mother had more money than you, so why would she borrow money from you?"

"It's a long story."

"It's going to be longer than you think. Now I know why you want my good will. You know damn well that these supposed transactions have no leg to stand on in a court of law."

"I know more about the law than you do, young effendi."

"Well, you old governor. We'll see."

And so the flames of war were fanned between the old governor and the young effendi. That was how they referred to each other. Ahmed Pasha would say to Omar, "You tell the young effendi that if he doesn't tell that fool lawyer of his to not refer to me in this manner in the documents he sends me, I will ruin him."

When Omar had delivered that message, Khaled would answer with a laugh, "Easy there, easy. Tell the old governor death comes to us all. He hasn't seen anything yet. We still have the great performance, the grand opening of the next judicial season. Perhaps you don't know that your father, the old governor, didn't have the time for more subtle maneuvers and had resorted to forgery. Outright forgery. Go tell him that. Maybe it will keep him up tonight."

And so the fire raged hotter and the trials multiplied between father and son. Or let's say the effendi and the governor, so we don't anger one or the other. If one of them sued, the other sued twice over. If one hired a lawyer of the rank of bey, the other found one at the rank of pasha. If they drafted a claim, they insisted on giving copies to all their family and friends.

They loved their lawsuits the way mothers love their infants. They waited for the rulings like a fasting man waits for sunset. They expended all their strength to keep up with the latest news on the various claims. One time, a final sentence was delayed until three in the afternoon. Ahmed Pasha could not eat. He waited by the phone until he heard the judge's decision. As for Khaled, he had gone to the courthouse at eight o'clock that morning and sat there waiting for the decision for many a long hour. That particular decision was an interlocutory ruling in Khaled's favor. He took it upon himself to personally inform the old governor.

"And now you can eat with a good appetite, although it's probably a better idea to just go to your room and bury your worries in sleep. You say you suffer from insomnia? Well, I am happy to tell you there is a new drug out. It's extremely effective, and will give you some peace. Would you like me to tell you its name, or—"

But Ahmed Pasha showered his son with as many insults as he could think of, and then hung up.

It was a strange thing, really, that Khaled, who cared nothing for money, should be so invested in these suits against his father. But when he was asked, he had a clear answer: "These claims against the old governor are not mine; they are in reality the claims of society. I am merely the instrument. Society benefits enormously if the old governor is impoverished. And it loses much if he is made wealthy. Indeed, the old governor himself would be improved by the total loss of his wealth."

Khaled had no resources for these expensive court cases, of course, and so there was no choice but to collude with the enemy, who were more than happy to oblige. And those enemies, after all, were none other than his aunts, his father's sisters. The issue was personal to them, since they hated his father as much as he did. They fanned the flames of war as much as he did. He chose one of them, and took up residence at her house. She was the least like his father. That was her first advantage in Khaled's eyes. The second was that she was a widow who had only one daughter, a charming young woman by the name of Niamat. Niamat had beautiful shapely arms, which she insisted on leaving uncovered. And for that reason, Khaled had no option but to set up residence with this very aunt.

Khaled's story at this point was simply one of various legal developments in the battle between him and his father. This battle raged on from year to year, and no final decision was reached on any claim. On the contrary, the claims grew and multiplied, and spread to all the courts of the land.

But stories about the law are joyless. Let's leave Khaled to his solitude and legal struggles, and revisit him two years down the line to see what had become of him, and of Malim.

Part 2

# 7

In the Khayamiya neighborhood, there is an ancient corner known as the Citadel. Now, this Citadel was once a palace belonging to one of the Mamluks. Or, to be more accurate, it was a large house, which the owner referred to as a palace, because its owner was a Mamluk, and a Mamluk cannot live in anything that is not a palace. It had nothing of the markings of a palace except for an enormous wooden door, leading to a dark vestibule, and then an atrium with a granite pool. Perhaps the Mamluk used to fill that pool with water. Perhaps he would sit there before sunset among his followers and clap, whereupon he would be brought a hookah prepared specially for him. And there he would be a sultan for a while.

There is no doubt, of course, that he was killed by poison or daggers, because he was a Mamluk, and Mamluks, for some unknown reason, didn't die natural deaths. And then maybe his enemy took possession of the palace, after he had killed his children and married his wife, as was the custom at the time. And after that a lot of killing must have happened, and as many marriages. We can surmise this because we know that marriage for a lot of people doesn't remove the ill will caused by murder (except perhaps among the youngest widows). And so the citizens of the Khayamiya in the twentieth century were convinced that the palace was haunted by a crowd of evil spirits. Spirits ran wantonly through the palace in the middle of the night, and filled it with screams and cries. Stories spread quickly, crafted by the idle tongues of the weavers in the district. And while these stories occupied them, they condemned the building to standing completely unused.

Then there was the fact that the palace was the responsibility of the Ministry of Endowments, and this increased the number of evil spirits that haunted it, and so the palace sat there, abandoned.

And while the ministry scratched its head, bewildered by this cursed palace, it was visited by a young man by the name of Nasif, who asked to rent it for two pounds a month, for a period of three years. Ten spacious rooms, not to mention the enormous wooden door and the granite pool, all for two pounds a month. A good deal. But they still thought the boy was mentally deficient, or at the very least a fool. Were he to agree to be paid two pounds a night to live in that place, he would still be the losing party. In fact, an open wager for the value of five pounds was public at that time: anyone who agreed to spend a night in the Mamluk palace would win this sum. There were no takers.

Nasif, however, did not care about these terrifying rumors. He had absolutely zero interest in confirming or

denying them. Spirits had become a naive supe/
him, since he—in his heroic path of self-educa..
managed to free himself from an even more popular, and
more feasible, superstition. For Nasif professed a religion
revealed by a prophet named Zarathustra, and for this reason Nasif believed that he created himself, and the world.
Of course, when he sorted through his memory for examples
of what he had created, he couldn't recall creating anything
called a spirit. And so, in his world at least, there was no
such thing as spirits. In the world of others, spirits could exist
perhaps, since they created these useless things with a lot of
effort. A certain type of person created not only spirits, but
all kinds of masters, because they sought to be ruled, and not
to rule. A man could either take the whip or be whipped, and
most people preferred to be whipped because they were then
freed of the responsibility of the arduous task of whipping.
These were people who denied their humanity and fled it.
For struggle and whipping and control were the reasons man
created himself. Thus spake Zarathustra.

For this reason, Nasif found an intense pleasure in establishing his own Citadel in a structure that he pillaged from
some of the slave drivers of humanity. In this way he took
away their whips, and flogged them with them. In fact, he
found more in it than pleasure: he found utility.

Nasif was not unemployed. Although he did not have
a particular occupation, he was occupied with enjoying life
as a whole. As for employees and bureaucrats, they were the

truly idle, for they turned away from life in ways no different from imbibing opium. They were idle because they stilled the workings of their mind, and restrained it from flying. Instead, they reined it in and put it to use counting the number of minutes a particular employee was late in any given month, or the amount of blood a doctor needed to leech from his patients before he could become rich. As for the men of thought, they sat at their desks eight hours a day wondering whether man created evil or whether evil existed before the creation of man. And as for those scholars whose minds escaped their control: that was where suicide statistics went through the roof and the number of inmates increased at local psychiatric institutions.

Humanity, according to Nasif, should never put up with this sort of idleness except for the bare minimum required to plant a seed or adjust a machine. This sort of idleness was a price all needed to pay to fulfill their needs. It would decrease, this price, as technology progressed, until there was almost nothing left to pay. A day would come when people would be idle like this no more than a handful of minutes a day, with the rest of their time spent in the noble pursuit of intellectual questing.

But Nasif was not a mechanic or a farmer. He wasn't rich either. And so he rented the Citadel and gave himself the best and most spacious room, at the very top. As for the rest of the rooms, he rented them out to varying types of people, charging between a pound and a pound and a half for each room. He had no difficulty in finding renters. He knew exactly whom to approach.

He knew this, because the Citadel was in a neighborhood considered a model Eastern neighborhood. It was the kind of neighborhood that attracted tourists from the four corners of the world. The scenes one came across were like those found in colored pictures in stationery stores above the legend: "A Souvenir from Egypt." If you walked down Taht al-Ruba Street and went around the corner into the Khayamiya neighborhood, you would find yourself in a street roofed with wood. The regular square openings in that roof let through sunlight like threads of gold and silver. It was as if you were seeing not a real world, but an image from some dream. This was where Hassan the Clever lived, and his beloved, Qamar al-Zaman, would watch him from that arabesque lattice over there. Sindbad lived across the street from her house. And as for Hassan the Fisherman, he lived next door. Here was where you could find all those characters from the *Arabian Nights*, which you read about but could never locate. Here you could see all those vistas of the imagination that became symbolic of the whole world of the magic of the East and its mystery. And the marketplace was center stage: small stores on either side of you; a craftsman with a hammer, beating away; a seller standing over his wares, crying out; canvas makers and the leatherworkers. In this little shop you could eat the tastiest little pies, and over on that side was the most skilled maker of malt beverages. It was complete chaos. Cries rose up on every side, mixed with the sounds of hammering and the ringing of various metals. Women wrapped in silk swayed as they walked and their dark eyes gleamed behind their veils. The crowds could not restrain their admiration, and shouted after them, "Like a full moon!" and "Pasha!" A glance behind you, and there stood the Metwalli Gate, filled with secrets. It had seen the entire history of the Cairo of al-Muiz, Capital of the East and Princess of Cities.

What kind of evil spirit could stand in the way of an individual capable of exploiting all this magic? The only difficulty lay in pinpointing those susceptible to this form of sorcery. For the general Egyptian populace, the neighborhood of Khayamiya was counted among the "provincial poor neighborhoods." It offended them with its filth and its low quality of life. That was why half of Nasif's Citadel renters were foreigners, and the other half were those who saw their own country through the eyes of foreigners. All of them were employed in the arts, or literature, or journalism. And there was a carpenter and a barber in that crowd for some reason. But perhaps they too were in some way connected to the arts, for the carpenter always wore a jet-black galabiya decorated with gleaming seashells, and the barber sported long sideburns and had an oud upon which he would play one or two tunes, every now and then.

In short, the Citadel gathered the strangest group of people within the walls of one house. And perhaps the strangest thing was the fact that among them were Malim and his father, the Madman of Housh Eisa.

*

Malim left prison the same month his father was released. He was unemployed for a while, and then he worked at one of the cafés that were his father's theater of operations for a while. Nasif saw him there. He'd known Malim from before, and so offered him a job. The Citadel project had begun in earnest then, and Malim said to him, "You might change your mind when you find out I've become a prison graduate."

But Nasif answered, "That's why I picked you."

"Even though my crime was theft?"

"I don't have anything for you to steal. Listen, have you been to school at any point?"

Malim looked at him in amazement. "I've never set foot in a school in my life."

Nasif nodded. "That's why," he said.

This was just something Nasif did. He asked any boy he saw this question, and, regardless of the answer, whether they said yes or no, he would nod and say, "That's why."

So Malim took the job with Nasif, and took his dog, Fido, with him. He had found Fido when he left prison, lying peacefully in front of the door of their home as if nothing at all had happened. When they arrived at the Citadel, Malim loved it immediately. He knew that he had once more found his old, free world in this ancient house. He built his dog a small doghouse and placed it in the corridor next to the door to his room. On the other side of the door, he made up a bed for himself. Having done this, he set off and ranged over the whole Citadel putting everything in order and setting right its affairs, until it began to resemble a sort of inn, the kind supervised by an excellent Swiss manager. He didn't like the bareness of the atrium, so he planted some plants and flowers in it. With the help of the carpenter, he set up a lattice and covered it with vines. And the pool was now filled with water, in which little red fishes swam.

The residents of the Citadel now felt that things had really turned around. Their residency in that old house was a real pleasure, whereas they had at first felt it was somewhat of a disappointment. Most of them, after a month or two, had stopped living there all the time. Some of them began to think of it as an ivory tower: they took to it when they felt the need for solitude. Others used it as a lovers' den: they took refuge in it whenever they had no other option. The artists turned their rooms into studios, which they only visited when they wished to paint or sculpt.

For a while, Nasif felt his project failing. But he knew a foreigner, a woman painter, who called herself Haniya. This Haniya had no known citizenship. Sometimes she was Polish, sometimes Hungarian, and sometimes, if necessary, Russian. She was a slender girl, petite, blonde, and with blue eyes that gave off a strange glow that cast her face in a charming light. She had arrived in Egypt five years ago, expecting to be famous and rich within a short time. But fate would not have it, and her exhibitions did not meet with any acceptance from the general public. And so she found herself poorer than when she arrived, and was forced in the end to give painting lessons to the daughters of the wealthy. The fact is, the girl had no talent. Her style was immature and limited, the colors she used were garish and disturbed, and the paintings showed an incorrect understanding of light and shadow. And perhaps her subconscious mind—that kindly old man who always seeks to soften the blow of our stupidity—managed to convince her, from some unknown location, that she would not do well at this particular sort of painting. So she turned to surrealism. This is a school of painting that makes of the subconscious a major prophet, with knowledge of all things in existence and of its secrets. The paintings of these artists sometimes contained impressive insights. For the most part, however, they were closer to a storage room full of old trash, or perhaps to a secondhand store. They seemed to be missing that essential unity of a work of art. Instead of a whole in which each part sheds light on the other, the work of art becomes a sort of barren plot of land that contains things that resist and reject each other.

So Haniya painted paintings that people did not understand, and that Haniya did not understand. One could say the paintings did not understand themselves.

Nasif tempted this young woman with a stay at the Citadel. She didn't hesitate, since she had no family in Egypt. Her arrival caused a stir among the Citadel's residents. They became enamored of the place. Each of them considered himself the knight who would be able to steal the heart of the lady. But Haniya did not pay much heed to her painterly companions. They in turn did not much care about her opinions on art theory. Nobody pays much attention, really, to female painters' opinions on art theory.

And so the residents of the Citadel went back to their old ways, and stayed that way until Malim appeared on the stage, with the Madman of Housh Eisa. That silent young man turned that building on the verge of collapse into a lively meeting place where people could find anything they needed. There was food and drink. There were places that were pleasant to sit in. There was joy and playfulness and a community spirit. There was a limitless freedom and precise order at one and the same time. The Madman was a constant source of entertainment. And, most of all, there was Malim. That magical, mysterious young man who ruled their hearts.

As the days passed, Malim became the only means through which anything could be achieved in the Citadel. Whenever the Comrade Bastards, as the residents of the Citadel came to call themselves, wanted to buy something they sent Malim. Malim made their deals, Malim managed their affairs, Malim solved their problems, and no one but Malim could successfully get them out of any crisis they managed to get themselves into. Malim mixed their paints, prepared their pens and inkwells, and sourced the stones and tools for their sculptures.

One day, as the Comrades were sitting around sipping wine, Haniya called out to Malim. Saad, who worked at one of the weekly magazines, and who was sitting right next to her, exploded with laughter. "Maybe you want Malim to drink your wine for you, too," he said.

"You're drunk, Saad."

"It stands to reason. It's not possible, for example, that I would be the one drinking and Malim would be the one getting drunk, is it? But you are wiser than me, Haniya. Malim will drink, and you will get drunk without wine."

Khoren, an Egyptianized Armenian, took advantage of this opportunity to get involved. His father had made a fortune making shoes, but Khoren had felt an artistic impulse in his core. Making do with what wealth his father had accumulated, he chose to come to the Citadel to learn the craft of painting at the feet of Haniya.

"You're wrong, Saad," Khoren said. "Haniya gets drunk on the wine of Malim."

"I absolutely forbid you to make these crude remarks," she replied sharply.

Saad laughed. "Don't be angry, Haniya," he said. "The truth is, Malim has become a husband to all of us."

But she did not like these remarks. Or perhaps she did not want her silence to be seen as consent, so she said with determination, "Malim is just a servant."

Now Nasif spoke—he was always the last to speak. "That," he said, "is a revaluation of values. Today, Malim is the master of the Citadel."

But the woman held to her views. "He's pathetic," she said.

"He is an exceptional person," Saad said, and then added, "and I have no compunction about telling you, Comrades, that I respect him more than I respect myself."

Nasif had no choice at this point but to make clear: "He is neither pathetic nor exceptional. He is normal. And that is why he has such power over you. Because we, Comrades, are failures. As for Malim, he is effective. If he had been working in the house of a merchant, say, or government employee, he would be just a servant, as you put it, Haniya, since those men are considered successful in the society we live in. Working for them, Malim would be in his natural position. As for us: we are rejects. We are a false note in the melody of society. People do not value us. They despise us. This is natural, and we expect nothing else. Where we are truly to blame is that we do not value ourselves. At the very core of each of us, there is a vast question: is society perhaps right? We don't really trust ourselves. That is the sole reason Malim has grown so enormous in our eyes; the reason he's taken on the proportions of a mythological creature."

Here Saad interjected, saying, "I swear you read the story I wrote about him! That phrase, that very phrase, 'the proportions of a mythological creature,' is in the text word for word!"

Haniya laughed. "It seems that we have all taken Malim as the subject of our art. I have made a painting of him entitled 'Master Malim' and was going to show it to you tomorrow."

"I thought you said he was just a servant," said Khoren with some irony.

"He is a master in images only."

"My dear girl," said Nasif, with a shake of his head, "what are we but images? This Citadel of ours itself is nothing but an image cast away on the side of the road."

He had barely finished this discourse when Mr. Shatta approached in some haste. "Don't panic, Comrades! Very soon we will hold the reins of power in our hands. Today I heard a worker say, 'These parliamentarians make laws only for themselves.' Our opinions have made their way into the hearts of the people. All we need now is the spark to start the blaze! This is why I ran here to you, to prepare, so we are not taken by surprise. I am the head of government. Any objections? Haniya here, being a foreigner, gets the Ministry of Foreign Affairs."

This Mr. Shatta was a minor employee in the company of a foreigner who traded in cotton. That was the side of him he presented to society. But, as he was wont to say, he gave to that job only his fingernails and the tips of his hair. As for his hands and his head, those belonged to the real Mr. Shatta, the King of Egyptian Cinema. Soon to be. The truth, of course, was that Shatta had read a lot about cinema and the theater, but had never put his important knowledge to any actual use except on one occasion. He had once played a seller of iced licorice tea. Perhaps his acting in that role had penetrated his psyche, for he always walked with belly thrust out, hands out at his sides, and head raised, despite the fact that he was no longer carrying the tea dispenser. Despite all this, he was a very intelligent man, even if his knowledge of the cinema was superficial.

"My dear Comrade Bastards," said Shatta, "you know my theories about the art of lighting. Light and shadow, and light and shadow again is what I say. White curtains and black curtains. That is my theater. No seats, no tables. No doors, no windows. Lend me your ears. Still your hearts from beating, and your lungs from breathing. You will hear now the first act of my first play, performed in the theater of light and shadow. The name of the play is *The Magnificent Conman of Cairo*.

The Madman came to the Citadel when Malim's absences became more frequent: he would take Malim's place, and when he did so, he would stay by the door. Malim's absences became more frequent because he was no longer just a servant, he was now also the manager of a small independent business of sorts. His business, moreover, made the denizens of the Citadel a considerably larger income than any of them managed to make on their own. It also had the advantage of being easy, and not costing him the kinds of effort that contradicted his free nature, which balked at any restraints. It required only a brief walk, an hour or two in the afternoon, through the streets of Cairo. Let no one think that Malim was picking the pockets of innocent passersby during these walks. Rather, this work was a cunning arrangement that had come to him one day as he was playing with his dog, Fido. He went to Haniya first and asked her, but she refused to take part in it.

So he appealed to Nasif, who welcomed the idea and promised him that he would work at obtaining Haniya's consent.

He'd devised this stratagem when his position in the Citadel was under serious threat, although he was unaware of this fact. For some days before their conversation, Nasif had suggested a move, which the Comrades had rejected with much emotion.

He had said to them, "I would like to propose an experiment to prove to you that Malim is just a normal person. We fire him, and hire another servant. My wager is this: within two weeks he will have reached the same status among us that Malim has achieved."

The true motivation behind this was not the spirit of scientific investigation, as Nasif claimed. He was motivated by a kind of jealousy and envy. For the landlord of the Citadel took great pleasure in his leadership of the Comrade Bastards, in carrying the banner of intellectualism before them, in observing them from his high room with the gaze of a chief organizing a lesson or taking account. He liked to see them lower their voices so as not to disturb him as he thought out the plans for a brave new world. He liked the name "Nasif" to be, always, on the tips of their tongues.

But lately, he had come to the realization that Malim had snatched this chieftainship away. Attention had turned to Malim, and away from him. They painted pictures of him, carved statues of him, wrote stories about him. Master Malim. The Great Malim. And who knew what he would become next. Perhaps Nasif would sleep in the hallway, while Malim slept in the high bedroom of leadership. It was time he put a stop to this.

Malim's stratagem saved him from certain destruction. And it made them a lot of money.

# 8

THE TELEPHONE KEPT RINGING IN Khaled's room, relentlessly. He was deeply asleep, and woke up in a panic. When he had located the source of the disturbance, he lifted the receiver and placed it on the table. He closed his eyes and tried to go back to sleep. But instead of sleeping deeply, he began to dream that he was going to school, and that once he arrived, he discovered that he was barefoot. A group of students surrounded him and laughed at him. He felt more awake than asleep. He decided to just leave his bed, rather than fall prey to these boyhood dreams that had returned to him these past few days. He was always waking up anxious, worried, having just dreamed he was taking an examination and the time had run out and he hadn't written a single word and the proctor was calling out "Pens down!" and coming to take his paper. Khaled begged the proctor to grant him a moment in which he could write a sentence or two, but the man paid him no heed and snatched the paper away. Khaled cried. He followed the proctor, begging for mercy. Then he woke up. At other times, he was about to travel. He looked at his watch and discovered that there were only a few minutes before his train left, and he was still not dressed. He grabbed his clothes in a great hurry, tucked them under his arm, and raced to the train station, only to find the train had set off. He chased after it, shoving people out of the way, people who were looking at him in amazement and with mockery. He couldn't catch the train. It receded into the distance. He was standing in the train station, in his pajamas, and everyone was laughing at him.

He did not know why he was having these dreams. Was it a guilty conscience throwing up these images? Were they symbols for something he didn't understand? Maybe he really had failed the exam and missed the train.

He went to the window and pulled back the curtains. He looked at his watch. It was half past ten. His head felt heavy and his limbs weak, so he considered a cold shower. He considered some calisthenics. He thought about going to the balcony and breathing deeply. He wondered if the morning air would refresh him. He didn't do any of these things, and just threw himself into a chair beside his bed and lit a cigarette.

Things came full circle: the phone rang. He reached out lazily for the receiver, and answered, cigarette still in his mouth. A female voice asked, "Did you get married after you left us last night?"

He answered mechanically, not really thinking, "No. Did you?"

"If I got married, I wouldn't need to call you. Also, I didn't wake up at ten like you."

He answered irritably, "I didn't wake up at ten, young lady. It has been some three hours since I left my bed."

"Really! Well, I've called you three times, so why didn't you answer?"

"I was . . . I was reading. In the garden. It's utterly absurd that a man should waste these beautiful morning hours locked up in a room."

"Okay. Never mind. Did you know that you were the star of the party last night? Nobody could talk about anything else."

"It makes sense, since I was the only human being at that whole party."

"Oh? So you're not Superman after all?"

"No, I'm afraid my body still contains a stomach, just like the rest of you. And other parts you are not familiar with."

The woman cried out in French, "Incroyable!" and then raised her voice, talking to someone on the other side. "Zizi! Did you hear that? The Moulin Rouge has a stomach!"

Khaled snapped, "I told you not to call me that. It's not funny."

"You know very well, my dear, that when you go on and on, you are like a mill. You really should read Fisher, you know. Have you not read Fisher?"

"No, I only eat what he catches."

"Eat it! Does this stomach of yours eat books too?"

"What books?"

"Fisher's books. Do you not know Fisher, Khaled? He created Superman, you know."

Khaled sighed. Then he said, "Will you please just let me hang up?"

"No. Just wait a moment, I beg you. Are you coming to Hussein Bey's banquet this evening? He invited us yesterday after you left."

"The poor wretch."

"Will you come?"

"No."

"No! You can't be serious. Why not?"

"Because Hussein is my friend."

"Do you only attend the banquets of enemies?"

"Precisely. And I only live in the homes of enemies. I only live in the society of enemies, too."

"Well, if you don't go, I won't go."

"I doubt humanity will experience that as any great loss. Goodbye."

He hung up, and sat there thinking. He didn't know why he was so bothered by that conversation. But he felt the same way he did after the morning's dream. She had said that he was the star of last night's party. Perhaps it was because he had gone in loose gray trousers and an open cotton shirt, while everyone else was dressed in their best formal clothing, smelling of expensive perfume and glittering with jewels. He couldn't imagine that anyone would be impressed with him.

He was just a poor boy who went to school barefoot, while boys gathered around him, laughing.

His head was pounding. He called out to the servant to bring him a cup of coffee. There was a knock on the door, but it was not the servant. It was his cousin, Niamat. When he saw her he started to pretend to do something, but quickly realized he was helpless, and surrendered to his fate. One headache was enough. She approached him, saying, "Good morning, Khaled."

Khaled muttered something resembling a greeting and lit a new cigarette from the butt of the old.

The girl sat on the armrest of his chair and chided him. "No, no, no, Khaled. I'm not happy with you. You're fast becoming a tobacco addict. And you only started smoking a few weeks ago!"

Khaled muttered something that, when deciphered, suggested that his head hurt.

The young lady was silent for a while, and then asked, "Who were you talking to on the telephone this morning?"

So came the first sad, gentle notes. They would soon be followed by some minor chords, and then a full and lengthy lament. His fear of this performance was what had made him avoid Niamat for days on end. But he answered with that steady quality that only comes from long practice: "It was the tailor. I have yielded to your will and will soon have some fancy clothes, instead of those old ones you hate so much."

"Really? Oh, Khaled, now you deserve a kiss."

The poor wretch pursed his lips. There was no way out of the noose of those shapely arms. And in any case, a kiss was far preferable to the lament. But no more than a kiss. He stood up and released the shackle of shapely arms, saying, "Let me open the door to the balcony. Perhaps the bad air in here is what's causing my headache."

This was not a wise move. That embrace was the price for his being spared the lament. Having refused to pay the price, he would now have to suffer the abuse.

"No, Khaled Bey. The reason is not the bad air of the room. The reason is the bad environment you live in. The parties that last till dawn. Do you know what time you came in last night?"

"I didn't come home last night. I came home this morning. At two thirty." Khaled spoke reflexively, and immediately regretted it. His attitude toward Niamat for the past couple of months was a mystery to him. It had been that way since that one time, as they sat at the dining table, when he had remarked, "Niamat is an exceptional young lady."

His aunt had looked at him with a smile and said, "What a coincidence! She says the same of you. Pull yourself together then, and prepare for the wedding."

From that day on, it became clear that things were not going to stop at kisses, and he felt an intense aversion toward her, because, truth be told, those shapely arms were all that was attractive about his cousin. A soft, beautiful body. That was all. As for the girl who occupied that body, she was a bore. She

knew nothing about the world except what was absolutely necessary. She had spent her entire youth cooped up in this antique
house. Khaled was the first man she'd had any intimacy with,
and that was why she was all over him like the plague. Khaled
felt a warmth from her. But this warmth quickly turned to suf-
focation. She oppressed him. He fell in love with Niamat for
precisely one week. It wasn't even love, really. Just a sort of feeling of victory, a vanity. After one week, he did not even desire
her as a woman. The beautiful, shapely arms came to feel to
him like a cold serpent that made his skin crawl.

He fought against his feeling, and conveyed only affection
in front of the girl and his aunt. After all, he was living with
them, eating with them. The least he could do was play along,
as long as he was in their home. What's more, he was losing
confidence that this perennial legal battle between him and his
father would ever conclude. If his father defeated him the way
he had defeated Malim, then marrying Niamat was certainly
superior to homelessness.

He had to hedge his bets. And so, having answered her
sharply, he now drew close to her and bent his head, saying
with a note of deep regret, "Forgive me, Niamat. This headache has made me impatient."

But she wasn't just going to forgive him without giving her
tongue a round or two of exercise. "You are always impatient
in here, and very patient outside."

Khaled was not good with all this give and take. And in
any case he was a materialist, and the girl today had bared a

considerable portion of her chest. Her cheeks had a certain blush to them, and her eyes were particularly bright. Maybe she was a materialist as well, he thought, and he went ahead and practiced that philosophy.

Later, the girl was overwhelmed by this philosophy and asked him for forgiveness. Khaled got up, and she dragged him back down to her breasts, and spoke in that odd voice she affected when she was playing the role of the seductive woman who leads men astray. The voice required her to have sleepy eyes. "You didn't kiss me there, Dawlat," she said, using her pet name for him.

The very reason he was trying to escape was this request. And yet here he was, with his head between her shoulders, her palms directing him toward her breast, where she liked him to stick his lips. He kissed her twice. Three times. She didn't let go. He went back to kissing, but she was insatiable, and kept a firm hold on the back of his neck with one hand, while the other stroked his hair. Khaled was bored. His forehead began to sweat. While his lips closed and opened in a mechanical way, he was thinking about breakfast. Would his eggs be boiled or fried? He couldn't decide for a while, but finally decided on fried. The palms had finally released his head and their owner asked him, "Do you love me, Dawlat?"

Khaled, breakfast still on his mind, answered her, "I love them fried, Tutu."

The girl, still lying on the bed, went into fits of hysterical laughter. He stood there, bewildered. His mistake was not funny by any means. But the girl was always like this whenever they were intimate, laughing for no reason and at anything at all. This imbecilic laughter of hers was one of the reasons he despised her. He couldn't stand to look at her or hear her voice. He turned his back to her, went to the other side of the room, and uncovered a picture on which he was working. The drawing was still not finished. That same wild imagination that had driven him to wear Bedouin clothes had returned, and pressed into his hand some pastels. What a strange young man, this Khaled! If we could open his head, we would see two compartments. In one, we would see the twentieth century lying squarely in the middle, with its machines and equations. In the other, there would be the eighteenth century, gallivanting along in a forest through which a stream ran. But maybe everyone was like this, to one extent or another. Perhaps each man had two characters, and he would hesitate between them for a long time, before choosing one. Or not.

Khaled looked at the picture for a long minute. He heard the girl say, "When will you draw me, little Dawlat?"

When you're history, he thought. Out loud, he said, "Do you want to be drawn in your current state?"

She laughed. "You're naughty," she said.

"Go fix yourself up," he told her, "and then we will see about you."

"All right. I'll bring you your breakfast."

She got up, fixed her hair, and adjusted her clothes. She left the room, but only after a brief skirmish in which

Khaled suffered some kisses that landed on various locations on his head.

It wasn't fair, since he had already paid the price for getting rid of her earlier. But women are nothing if not excellent negotiators. Perhaps, too, the girl thought that whatever was between them gave her the right to accost him all day. She had made her intentions clear when she declared that she would bring him breakfast herself. This would be followed by a request to go down to the garden. Then maybe after that the cinema, or maybe out to the pyramids for the day, or Maadi. No doubt she was preparing a busy program that would not end before midnight.

The phone rang again. A female voice said, "Are you the mujahid?"

"Yes, Ratiba Hanem."

"Will you permit me a small question?"

"I wish I could. The mujahid is on a vacation that has lasted two years. I will alert you as soon as he begins to wage his jihad again."

All that was left was a quick escape, if he wanted to live a full life. Between the oppression of the domestic life, embodied in Niamat, and the threat of the outside world, embodied in the telephone, he might give up the ghost at any moment. And that was why he put on his clothes as quickly as he could and snuck out of the house, taking the servants' stairs, to walk the streets aimlessly.

# 9

KHALED SET OFF WITH NOWHERE in particular to go. All he wanted to do was avoid the areas where his friends gathered, and this led him finally to a garden by the banks of the Nile. Children were playing around him as he sat, and their nannies had settled in the shade of the trees, sewing or chatting.

How strange. It seemed to him that he had come to this place by sheer accident. And yet it was not the first time he had found himself in this garden. In fact, in this very seat. He had been here quite often. His feet seemed to lead him there whenever he was depressed, or oppressed by the world or his own self. At such times, he would find himself among these children, sitting in the shade of these trees, beside this river from the heart of Africa. He hated children. He hated gardens. Not even for a short time had he ever loved the Nile. What on earth could keep bringing him to this place?

This seemed to be the beginning of a spiritual crisis. He had the feeling that he was on the verge of another stage of his life. Perhaps he came to this hateful place to allow these suppressed emotions to rise to the surface and express themselves.

He spent the majority of his morning sitting there, looking at things dully and without comprehension. His sight would fall on a rose, and someone would have had to tell him it was a rose for him to understand what it was. His mind was pulled this way and that with thoughts of life and death. He paid these thoughts no heed, and simply allowed them to be until they were replaced by other thoughts. The depression did not leave him for a moment. But he thought of it without concern, as though it were a crisis someone else was suffering. He was not in a state to worry about someone else's crises. All he wanted to do was sit here like this, the way addicts slouched in a Shanghai opium den when the drug entered their bloodstream. Let this mind that had invaded his head think whatever it wanted. Let it imagine whatever fancies and wild imaginings it wanted to. It had nothing to do with him.

He woke from his delirium long after sunset, and found that the garden was empty. It was just him and that damn Nile, which seemed to him like the tail of Satan. He stood up and stumbled toward the door. He found a man selling pastries and bought one, making his way toward the city as he ate it. As he was crossing Qasr al-Nil Bridge, he felt a car stop next to him. He turned to find it filled with his friends, calling out to him to join them. He found himself shouting at them, cursing them, insulting them in phrases he had never uttered before in his life. Then he walked on, uncaring.

He found himself in Ismail Pasha Square. The crowd and noise bothered him, so he veered off into the side streets. Here it was calm. No one was around. Soon, a strange-looking dog began to circle him, coming up and then retreating, over and over again. He became impatient with the dog, and had drawn his leg back to kick him when he heard a voice saying, "Fido! Here boy!"

He turned and saw Malim.

They recognized one another immediately. Malim thought to himself that he had better get away, but he was too slow. Khaled had come running toward him, and Malim saw him stretch out his hand. Malim hesitated a moment, then held his hand out, and Khaled shook it warmly.

"How are you, Malim?"

"I'm all right. God's done well by me."

"When did you leave prison?"

"Six months ago."

Khaled looked at him awhile, then said, "You're much older now, Malim. Are you married yet?"

The young man laughed. "Sure," he said, "I have eight wives now."

"Eight! You must be rich, then, to sustain such a tribe."

"Actually, they pay me."

Khaled frowned and said, "What is it that you do exactly, Malim?"

Malim realized what Khaled was probably thinking and smiled. "It was just a joke, Khaled Bey," he said. "I'm not married."

Khaled insisted that they go to a nearby café. Malim agreed reluctantly, seeing the inevitability of a long conversation.

Over tea, Khaled began to express to him how sorry he was and how strong his desire was to make up for the sins of his father and his brother and to make things up to Malim for the time he spent in prison, for all the torture and persecution he must have experienced there. Malim thanked him gently and said he didn't require compensation, and that he hadn't been tortured in prison. It had been quite pleasant actually, for the most part. Khaled suggested that he could help Malim in any way that he needed, and Malim said he didn't need any help. To himself, Malim noted that he preferred the father's enmity to the son's help. The conversation was long and tedious. Khaled would not stop philosophizing or whining. Malim was impatient and bored, and wanted to get back to work.

Khaled continued his meditations for a while, and then said, "Isn't our meeting here today a stroke of good fortune? I had given up all hope of seeing you again. And now we are joined again by sheer coincidence. But I prefer not to think of it as coincidence. Or, if you like, you could say that coincidence is an essential part of a man's life, just like his planned actions. I could have searched and searched until I found you. Or I could have left it to sheer chance. It seems to be all the same."

Khaled liked this idea. He wouldn't let it go. It was as if he found pleasure in hearing his own voice. And while the Moulin Rouge ground out all these words, Malim had a thought: this fellow had completely wasted his time and what if he made him pay the price of that time? What if he added him to the list of marks he had worked over today?

His pockets contained only two cards, which was not exactly a record. Khaled's card could make a third, and then maybe he could obtain a fourth before he returned home. After all, Khaled's father had taken a year and a half out of his life. The least the son could do was pay him twenty piasters. It would not affect his budget much, after all.

Malim took advantage of a moment of silence (Khaled was swallowing) and blurted out, "Actually, Khaled Bey, our meeting wasn't exactly a coincidence."

"Oh? Were you looking for me?"

"No. But I am the messenger of someone who is. This person saw you today and sent me to you. I followed you for a while and was unsure whether to go ahead or leave you be. I knew who they were talking about as soon as they described you to me, and I'm not proud of the mission they gave me."

"This is all very strange, Malim. I don't understand a word of it."

"Do you go to Café Groppi often?"

"Unfortunately, and only because I have no other choice."

"This person also spends time there. That's where this person saw you."

"Who is this person, and how do you know them? You're being very mysterious. Did you do a course on politics in that prison?"

"If you knew my task, you wouldn't call me a politician. You'd call me something else entirely. I work for a foreign family. This family has a daughter who loves painting. This love has led her not to be very respectful of tradition. This in turn has led her parents to be very strict with her. This young woman saw you today passing by her home, and called me in quite a state, pointing at you. She insisted I give you a note. Naturally, I refused this job—which is not the job of a politician, as you thought—especially since I don't know you. But she begged me, and cried. When she saw on my face the signs of agreement she pushed me to the door, claiming to her parents that she had sent me to walk the dog."

Khaled listened thoughtfully to this monologue. He kept thinking for a long time, and then raised his head. "Is this lady of yours not tall, with dark, rather narrow eyes?"

Malim cried out excitedly. "So you do know her, Khaled Bey!" he said. "You've described her exactly."

"No, I don't know her. But a girl of that description used to frequent Groppi. She would often stare at me, but would turn away whenever our eyes met. I remember once I asked her to dance but she excused herself."

"She always does that. Refusing what is asked of her, even if she wants it, and asking for what is forbidden her, even when she doesn't really want it."

"What a weird girl. What's her message?"

"She asked me to find out your name and phone number. She also wants a time to call you."

"Okay. Tell her ten o'clock tomorrow morning." He took out his card and pushed it toward Malim, along with a silver coin.

**\***

Khaled went home with a brain full of dreams and torment. This foreign artist must be of a very different type than the girls he usually met. Perhaps her love would be the thing to pluck him out of the narrowness that had been oppressing him for the past couple of months. Perhaps she would be the one to resurrect him, return to him his energy, return him to the life struggle, make of him the man he had always wanted to be. And if she didn't do all that, then at least she would be an exciting romantic adventure. She would compensate for some of what he had suffered at the hands of Niamat.

This girl had appeared just in time. Khaled had become absolutely fed up with Egyptian women. He derived no pleasure from speaking with them. The Egyptian young woman was to him a medley of superficial thoughts, exhausting artificiality, and psychological complexes that irritated him greatly. She was just a female seeking a male mate. And if that were all, then perhaps he could have coped. But the Egyptian woman denied that she was just a female, and denied seeking a mate. To hide this, she pretended sometimes to be a young intellectual, at other times a young Europeanized woman who was very aware of the latest Western arts. Sometimes, too, she would be a reckless young woman, a freethinker, whereas in other circumstances it suited her to cast over her face the mask of conservatism and modesty. She was always acting out one role or another, in her failure to be herself. She was still in that primitive feminine state.

She had not yet become a human being. And it was going to be a long struggle for her.

These thoughts would not let him rest most of the night. He left his bed early the next morning. He shaved. He shaved again. He put on some clothes, took them off, put them on again. He did his hair, then styled it differently. He ran out of things to do and set up camp by the telephone and kept watch.

At precisely ten o'clock, the telephone rang. The impassioned lover picked up the receiver and asked who the speaker was. A soft feminine voice answered: "Is this Khaled Bey?"

"Yes."

The young woman told him that she didn't speak much Arabic, and asked if he knew German. He apologized and said he only knew English and a smattering of French. But, he added, "Your Arabic is wonderful, my lady. It is more beautiful when it comes from your lips."

"I like your voice, too. Malim said you knew me."

"I will, my lady. Passing glances are not knowledge."

"I want to know you, too."

"Why then did you refuse to dance with me when I asked you?"

"Because I . . . but I will tell you later, when we meet. I'm afraid my mother will come in at any moment."

"Well, I could meet you in Groppi in half an hour."

"Impossible. My mother would never agree that I go out at a time like this. Listen, Khaled Bey, I have a friend at 27 Qasr al-Nil Street, and opposite her lives an old woman who rents her apartment out for twenty piasters a night. I don't have that money now, so I will send Malim to you to get it from you. Does this make you angry?"

"No, lady, no! I am flying high with joy."

"Thank you, Khaled Bey. I have such a good feeling about our relationship. I'll wait for you by the door of the building I told you about at seven this evening. I'll wear a red rose."

"I already know what you look like, even without the rose. But you have not told me your name."

"You will know everything once we meet. Don't be late."

As per their agreement, he met Malim at the café they had met at before. Malim arrived promptly at five in the afternoon. Khaled asked him to sit for a moment, but Malim excused himself, saying that he had to return to his mistress as quickly as possible.

"Five minutes, no more."

"Please excuse me, Khaled Bey. The young mistress told me that you would give me a certain amount of money."

"Here it is. And this is for you."

Malim took the money from Khaled and hurried off. When he was a short distance away, he looked back, and then took off once more. Seeing this, Khaled had a strange feeling that things were not as they seemed. He got up immediately and pursued Malim.

He found him quickly, and followed him. It became apparent that he was not going to the house where he claimed to be employed. He was walking toward Fuad I Street, whereas the house he claimed to be working at was on Ismail Pasha Square. Khaled, naturally, became even more suspicious. Why exactly would Malim refuse to spend even a brief five minutes with him? Servants were routinely absent from their masters' homes for hours and hours. And why was Malim so eager for the money, as though it were personally important to him, as though he feared Khaled would not give it to him?

He thought back to the conversation between him and the foreign girl. In light of his new suspicions, there were things he could not explain. When the girl had sprung on him this room business, he had assumed that she did what she liked because she did not have a duplicitous nature. But it seemed strange to him now that the first meeting between him and a girl should be in a private room, with a bed. That went against the very nature of sound romantic affairs. Beds were not a prolegomenon. They were a conclusion. And what was that business with the red rose? She said she knew him, and he said he knew her.

While he was speculating, he saw Malim shyly approaching a young man standing at a shop window.

He saw them speak briefly, a conversation that ended with the young man giving Malim his card, on which he wrote something, and a small amount of money. Malim thanked him and went on his way.

Khaled followed. They finally reached Fuad I Street and there Malim waited for the tram. Khaled was surprised to see him get on the number thirteen tram headed toward the neighborhoods of New Hilmiya and the Citadel. Who could imagine that his foreign mistress lived in such an area? Khaled jumped into the tram, determined to follow this story to its end. At the very least, it was an interesting adventure. When the tram reached Bab al-Khalq Square, Malim disembarked, and Khaled followed suit. He saw Malim cross the square and turn into Bab al-Ruba, and was even more surprised.

It seemed that the people on the street all knew Malim. He hardly took a step without returning someone's greeting. He kept walking until he reached the Metwalli Gate and turned right and went into Khayamiya Street, which was crowded with people through whom he skillfully and nimbly waded. When the people of the neighborhood saw him, they began to call out to him. "Hey, Malim . . ." and "Come here, Malim . . ." But he didn't go over to them, he just waved and called out greetings, or made a quick joke, or snatched a cucumber from a street seller's cart. A young woman wrapped in a black shawl glanced at him lazily and drawled, "What a beautiful man you are."

He took the tip of her chin in his fingers. "Wait till you're a bit older, Fathiya. Not long ago you were still just a little girl."

The young woman swayed in front of him. "Well, I'm grown up now, Malim," she pointed out. "What more do you want?"

She said this and let her shawl fall a little to show a chest as smooth and shapely and firm as a marble statue.

But Malim covered her shoulder. "All right then," he joked, "wait till *I* grow up."

He left the girl and went into a shop and the owner made two pies covered in ghee for him and slipped them into the oven. They came out looking for all the world like two perfect flowers, and he sprinkled them with rose water and sugar. Malim took them and skipped down to the Citadel. He knocked in an elaborate rhythm and the door opened, and then he shut it behind him immediately.

He simply disappeared into the darkness, as if he were a dream.

# 10

MALIM WENT INTO HANIYA'S ROOM without knocking. She was looking out of the window, and she stayed like that with her back to him. Her room was split into two sections. On one side were a bed and a desk covered with books and papers. On the other side was a frame with a canvas on it and painting utensils.

Malim walked slowly toward her. When he was halfway across the room she said, "I didn't hear you knock."

"True."

"So go out and knock and don't come back in until I give you permission."

"All right."

He turned to go, but she spoke again. "I forbid you to come in here without knocking. Do you hear me?"

"I hear you."

He started moving toward the door again, but Haniya cried out, "Where are you going? Come here and tell me who that girl you were flirting with is? I was watching you, so don't try to deny it."

"It was Fathiya."

"I don't give a damn if it was Fathiya or Fatma! Of course that's the type of girl you would want. You're just a low-class street urchin. I don't even know why you came up here. Go back down to her. What are you waiting for?"

Malim didn't seem to be hurt by these attacks. He answered her serenely: "I came to give you your cut. I have two cards and sixty piasters."

"I don't want your cards or your money. You go and tell that scam artist Nasif that I will no longer play this role you have forced upon me. Do you take me for one of those whores you meet in bars? You, and your boss, and everyone in this damn Citadel are nothing but scum. All this talk of art and literature is nothing but a cover. It's a cover for their disgusting actions. It's like one of those masks thieves wear to cover their faces during a robbery. It's time you understood that I am not like you. I am really at a loss about all those who call themselves radicals in this country. I've traveled all over Europe, you know, and I've mingled with artists in every country. Never in my life have I seen anything like this hellish Citadel and the duplicitous bastards who live in it. And the worst thing is, they hand over leadership to a lowlife like you. No! I'm not like you. And I'm leaving tomorrow morning."

Malim was distracted by counting the money in his pocket. He was testing a silver piece, suspicious of its quality. He had begun to tap it gently against the floor to make sure, but when he heard the girl threatening to leave, he became alert. He reached out and grabbed her arm roughly. "You're not leaving."

She looked at him disdainfully. "And who, Your Highness Prince Malim, is going to stop me?"

He grabbed her other arm and repeated, "You're not leaving. You're staying right here."

She didn't try to escape his grip. Instead, she seemed frail and broken now. "What difference does it make to you if I stay or if I go?" she asked. "As long as you have Fathiya by your side?"

"You know how many jobs I've been offered. Jobs for more money, jobs with more dignity. But I refused all of them. I preferred to stay here, a homeless servant, just to be by your side. I serve everyone in this house, not just you. But when I came up with this scam, I didn't do it for Nasif like you accuse me. I did it for you. I heard you saying you wanted a new dress and didn't have the money. No. You're not going anywhere."

It wasn't Malim's habit to give speeches. He mainly expressed himself in a phrase or two. It was the first time Haniya had heard him say so much. His severity and confidence, and the control he had over his words, worked to soften her heart. It had been a long time since she had heard a true man speak. The people of the Citadel only ever spoke with "perhaps" and "it may be the case." Malim simply said, "No."

She looked at him a long time, and then said, "You're tired, Malim."

And he let go her arm and said, "Yes. I walked a lot today."

"It makes me happy that you exhaust yourself for me. You are the only one who takes care of me."

Malim lit the cigarette he had brought with him. "I brought you those pies you like," he said.

Haniya laughed. "Thank you, Malim. I told you: you're the only one who takes care of me. Come, let's eat them together."

"I'm going to bathe. I need to wash the sweat of scams and hustling off me. Dishonorable work is as hard as honorable work, it seems. It's just less boring."

Haniya clapped. "What an excellent student you are," she said. "You're talking just like them. All that's left is for you to take that final step and say that there is no difference between honorable and dishonorable work. To say that they are both simply a means to an end. To say that it's just a matter of whether you succeed or not."

Malim frowned for a while, and then replied, "No. Some work really is shameful. Would you like it if I didn't give that baker what I owed him for those pies?"

"You forget the money you took from your poor victims today."

"Those are the crumbs of what they have. That baker eats from what he earns. If I take a piaster from him, his family eats one less loaf."

Haniya laughed. "You see? An excellent student."

"Here's your cut. Thirty piasters. The other thirty are for Nasif. He gets the fake one. As for me, Khaled Bey gave me ten piasters, and that other young man gave five."

She reached out and took the card, and then gave it back to him. "It's in Arabic," she said. "Read it, Malim."

Malim read it with some difficulty. "Muhsin Abdel-Baqi, Social Worker. So he is idle. This one will show up here soon. We really need a social worker."

"Don't worry about that. Someone like that arrived today. What a bore. He looks like one of those Spanish matadors."

"Is he a social worker too?"

"Something like that . . . Oh, no, I remember. He's a therapist. He came in with a puffed-up chest, like a rooster. He had an absurd gait, like a goose. He walked like this to where we were sitting in the shade and stood in a Napoleonic sort of posture, which of course made his chest puff out even more. He gazed at us, looking from one side to the other for a while, and then he spoke. He used all the muscles of his respiratory system, so you felt he would explode with the amount of air he had stored up. Then he blared out, 'Mr. Nasif!' I almost burst out laughing. It was obvious that he had rehearsed this for some time. Things went quiet for a second. We were all thinking about this natural disaster that had appeared before us all of a sudden. I was the first to speak. I inhaled, stored as much air as I could in my lungs, squeezed my throat as tightly as I could, and then said, in my best approximation of his voice, 'Mr. Nasif is dead!' That's when everyone laughed. But our guest just raised his nose high in the air and gazed down at us, like they do in the movies. He didn't last long, though. He was kind of disturbed. He didn't really expect that kind of reception. He started muttering, 'What? What is this!' until Nasif took pity on him and invited him to sit."

Malim was laughing hard. "Brilliant," he said.

"Oh, you should have seen him, Malim, when he said hello. He came up to me majestically. He knelt in front of me, like a knight from the Middle Ages. I think he was waiting for me to extend my hand. He kept referring to me as 'the respected mademoiselle.' It was like he was reading me an old letter."

"Where is he now?"

"He's probably sitting with them. I knew you were coming, so I left. Tell me, how did it go with Khaled? You were really scared of meeting him!"

"Yes. He said he wanted to help me and set me on the right path. These good intentions of his are my biggest fear in life."

Haniya threw herself on the bed. "I'm so tired, Malim," she said. "Come sit next to me. I want to tell you something."

Malim began to do as she asked, but suddenly stopped. The sound of violent knocking rang through the Citadel, tearing the serenity of the night to shreds.

Khaled had never been to this place before. Actually, he could not have imagined that there was even such a place as this neighborhood to which Malim had led him. When he reached that part of the street with the wooden lattice roof, the feeling of disbelief grew. He felt as though he had found an Eastern capital—Damascus, say, or Baghdad, or Bombay. Not Cairo, though. It seemed to him that the people he saw around him were not the Egyptians he knew. Their faces, while Eastern of course, were nevertheless strange. It was as if these were the faces of people from a distant land to the west—Morocco perhaps, or from the other direction, say, Persia.

He became afraid at first, among these people, following Malim. The people around him seemed like predators as they watched him with their suspicious gazes. Who knew for sure that they would not gather around him and beat him or rob him, or at the very least humiliate him for their entertainment? What was he to do? What could he possibly do to push back against their aggression? He could not understand their language, after all, nor they his.

How strange. How strange that this could be the home of that foreign girl with whom he had spoken just that morning. Was she the head of some gang? But women do not lead gangs except in children's stories. A spy then. She was a spy who knew that he was estranged from his father, and she wanted to mine him for information. She was living in this place so she would go unnoticed.

While he mulled these thoughts over, Malim disappeared into the crowds. Khaled ran to where he saw him last, and looked around futilely. Where had that devil gone? He must be far ahead of him. That boy was as nimble as a butterfly: he seemed to be floating above people as he went. He quickened his pace, looking right and left, but could find no trace of him. He thought he should go back to where he started. He went all the way back to the Metwalli Gate but still could not see that spirit, Malim. And then an opportunity fell into his lap. Khaled stood in front of the gate for a while, looking into its dark recesses. It was like a dark cave, which people came out of only to steal and rob others. Khaled felt an intense hatred of himself. Was he really that cowardly? These passersby, not just the men but the women and even the children—all of them were stouter of heart than he was. They were stronger than him. He was closer to despair than he was to struggle. He had no tricks, and was quick to lay down his arms.

He strengthened his resolve. He would do it even if he had to talk to these foreigners who lived in this neighborhood. After all, did they not have to abide by Egyptian laws? So, they could not beat him or rob him. And in any case they were human beings after all, and Easterners too. They would not shun a stranger.

Khaled went back to the Khayamiya district. He looked for someone who had a kindly face and a gentle nature. That long search finally led him to a seller of guavas. He presented himself, asked to buy guavas, and did not haggle over the price. While the man weighed out the fruit, Khaled asked him, "Do you know Malim?"

"Who doesn't know that little son of a bitch?" the man answered. "He was just here a minute ago."

"Do you know where he lives?"

The man looked at him suspiciously. "Strange," he said. "Are you not one of them?"

"Who?"

"Those effendis and foreigners that Malim works for."

"No. One of them is a friend of mine, but I can't find the house they live in."

"Here are your guavas. It's the third door on the right."

Khaled took the fruit and went down to the house. He saw before him a huge door, foreboding. It did not invite knocking or welcome guests. He became afraid once more. How could he knock on the door of people he did not know, this late at night? Assuming they opened, what would he say? What had happened between him and Malim was closer to fantasy than to fact. They would laugh at him until they spilled their guts on the floor. And what was he going to do with these guavas?

He would eat them. Khaled sat down on the threshold, took a guava, and bit into it. He didn't like it, so he tossed it and took another one. But before his teeth bit into the second one, he found himself throwing the whole bag to the ground. He leapt up suddenly and began to pound on the door, violently.

# 11

THE NEWCOMER EXHALED THE smoke from his cigarette in stages. Then he began speaking.

"We are like someone curating an exhibition of oil paintings in the middle of a barren desert. And who then asks the nomads to patronize it. The desert won't ever stop being a desert in this way, nor will the art of painting become finer because some Bedouins visit it. No, gentlemen. We have no need for literature or art. We need labor. Bold, decisive labor. What good has it done the East, all this poetry that its poets have produced across the ages? None. None save the fact that the word 'East' has come to be synonymous with fairy tales and delusions. The poetry of the East is like an opiate imbibed by a lazy failure of a man. We recite poetry because we are incapable of work. If we rise, if we innovate a new civic culture, a new, modern people, we wouldn't recite any poetry. But if we keep reciting poems, we will not rise. And so, it is my opinion that we take the initiative and hurry to work. Never mind all this painting of pictures and composing of articles."

The newcomer's name was Atallah. That was the only name on his card. Just Atallah. No title, no surname. As if it were the business card of Abul-Alaa, say, or Socrates. It seemed he was one of those types that liked the sound of his own voice. He talked a lot, interrupted a lot, listened very little. Saad listened to him wearily and with boredom. He had disliked him the minute he laid eyes on him, actually. That was why he led the resistance among the Comrade Bastards. He never let Atallah get away with anything without vigorous debate. He took a position opposing Atallah, irrespective of what that position might be.

And that was why he turned to him, and challenged: "Mr. Atallah. Your opinion—being an opinion—is worthy of respect. But, like any argument, it ultimately obliterates itself. You say that our people have not yet developed a mature consciousness, so there is no point in composing poetry or prose for such a people. But, I ask you, how is an ignorant people to rise up if it does not read prose or listen to poetry? The fundamental requirement of any reform is to create a social consciousness. Without such a consciousness, the farmer does not know he is oppressed, nor the factory worker that he is exploited. So, I ask you again, how do we form such a consciousness without literature or art?"

Atallah tried to interrupt Saad after each sentence. Saad would raise his voice to defeat him. Atallah would then in turn raise his voice to put a stop to Atallah. By the time Saad was finished they were both shouting at the tops of their voices, as though they were fighting.

Shatta, in the meantime, had taken a corner in the shade, alone, drinking wine out of a bottle. All this shouting was hurting his mood. He was roaming through wine-induced fantasies. He started shouting at them: "Take it easy on yourselves. Or at least take it easy on us. Your voices are too much for our ears. I swear the two of you alone are enough to ruin any movie script. This is not how dialogue is done. Interruption, Mr. Atallah, is an art. You should have learned it before you started practicing it. Also, you're using your esophagus completely wrong. You do not project. That's why you're all hoarse although you've only talked for an hour. It's a beginner's mistake. They—"

But Atallah did not let him finish. He just pushed ahead: "We don't need all this social-consciousness business! The people are just an obliging tool in the hands of skilled leaders. A capable leader can bring the dead to life! I ask *you*, Mr. Saad: were we in need of poetry when we carried out our nationalist revolution in 1919?"

"Well, if you had actually been in Rod al-Farag you would have known that political song was an essential element in fanning the flames of revolution in the spirits of the people. The 1919 revolution was only a success because of the social consciousness that had awakened through poetry. This is how the political inspiration spread even to the government employees, who are usually the last of the civil servants to revolt."

In this fashion, the Comrades continued with the give and take that was their habit in these interminable discussions. Such conversations never ended until someone lost their voice or

135

they all became hopelessly drunk. On this particular evening, however, Nasif insisted on silencing any of the members of his Citadel who went on at length when expressing their opinions. The Comrades understood the reasons for this, as did Atallah. Khoren was doing exactly this. Specifically, he was expounding on the one-party system, and how it did not contradict the spirit of democracy and how in fact it might be the ideal way for rule of the people by the people, and giving the examples of Turkey and Switzerland. But Nasif would not let him finish. He interrupted him abruptly: "No need to go on and on, Khoren. These are things we can all read about in books."

Here Atallah stood up, theatrical and comic enough to prompt Shatta to cry out from the depths of his being: "Silence, gentlemen! This is a wonderful dramatic moment. Raise your head a little more, Mr. Atallah. Start with a low voice, and raise it gradually until you reach a shout. Don't rush, or the effect will be lost and the scene will fail."

But, as usual, Atallah did not heed Mr. Shatta's advice. He spoke in that strained, broad voice of his. "I see, gentlemen," he said, "that you don't trust me. You think of me as an intruder into the movement. You should know, however, that I am one of the oldest freedom fighters in this country. I was fighting for reform while the rest of you were reading *Boys Magazine*. I have listened to your views and I find you all—except for Mr. Nasif, of course—to be rank beginners. Your principles are unsound and your opinions immature. You need guidance and direction. This is why I came to you when I heard of your movement. Expect no success if you are not supervised by a man hardened by battle experience and matured by the passage of time. I am that man."

Shatta could not help but cry out at this, wailing and lamenting. "Oh, woe, Mr. Atallah! You rushed it. You rushed it despite my warnings to you. And now you have turned a tragic scene into a farce."

Saad smiled. "Maybe that's the key to this character," he said. "He acts the knight, but the costume is a fool's."

As for Khoren, he felt that it was appropriate to rise to the defense of their guest. "Please, please, leave the man alone. Don't you recognize this man's long political struggle in mulids and local carnivals?"

"Oh, yes, yes!" Shatta yelled from a corner. "I remember now! Atallah would often set up a stand in the main mulids. It was quite a sight seeing him take his place on the stand in front of his stall, and around him the members of his revolutionary movement dressed in bright greens and reds. Quite colorful. There was a band, too, if I remember correctly. It was quite a sight. Where are you going, Mr. Atallah?"

Atallah was walking away with his goose-like walk toward the other end of the garden. Saad called out after him. "At the door you will find a person called the Madman of Housh Eisa. Take him with you, won't you? He is also one of those characters who are very useful to the movement."

But Atallah was not going to the door, as his detractors thought he would. He stood in the very center of the garden and called out, at the top of his voice, "Mr. Nasif! Permit me to speak with you privately."

Nasif was the only one who had not joined in the game. After sparking the conflagration, he had sat at some distance, watching and smiling. He felt something like victory. Here was a man who came to challenge him for leadership, and his followers had destroyed the newcomer without any effort from himself. His leadership was firm, because he was prudent. He had rented this Citadel and settled into it, patient, until his worth came to be known. In this way, his leadership had established itself over the Comrades.

Nasif looked at Atallah, who had adopted a stiff posture and raised his nose haughtily in the air, as a challenge to those who had dared offend him. It was very amusing, this Napoleonic stance of his, but Nasif did not laugh. He smiled. It was a smile of compassion and sympathy. He showed Atallah that he treated everyone equally, that he was above joining his comrades in their boyish play. Finally he spoke, in a voice overflowing with gentleness. "Please go ahead and say what you wish to say, Mr. Atallah," he said. "I have nothing to hide from the Comrades."

Nasif's good manners returned to Atallah some of his self-confidence, which, as always, expressed itself in arrogance and confrontation. He put his hand in his trouser pocket and stuck his chest out even more. Then he said, with some grandeur, "I have a message, and I have been asked to give it only to you, personally."

It struck Nasif that answering Atallah's call would raise his status with the Comrades. A private meeting with a messenger would give them the feeling that he was in contact with some influential parties. It would surround him with an air of mystery, a thing he was always careful to cultivate. When he went with Atallah, the Comrades would say to themselves, "I wonder what this message is that he is getting from unknown people? What is the source of the message? Nasif must be well known by people we have no knowledge of. . . ."

Nasif stood up with gravity and grace. He said, with the awesome voice of power, "Very well, Mr. Atallah. Let us retire to my chambers."

Nasif led the way, and Atallah followed in his wake. They went in this way up the dark wooden stairway without a word.

Atallah was having some difficulty finding his footing, and Nasif lit a match to help him see the way. Atallah felt a sense of terror. Their shadows danced on the walls like ghosts, like jinn, conspiring against them. They passed by a room with light glowing through the space at the bottom of its door. "Is that Haniya's room?" he asked.

"Yes," Nasif answered shortly.

"Who is that girl, really?"

"She's a foreigner."

"Is she in the movement?"

Nasif made an extra effort to enunciate his words. "She is just . . . a foreign . . . artist."

Atallah was quiet awhile. Then he said, "I don't know how long you are all going to withhold your trust from me. But maybe you'll change your mind when you read the letter."

Nasif turned the key in the lock and it screeched loudly. The door opened onto a dark room, and he lit another match and with it a huge oil lamp covered with a white glass shade. He made his way to his desk at one end of the room and stood in front of it, turning over the papers on the desk and riffling through them as though seeing them for the first time. It was a trick he used all the time, to give the impression that he was very busy and had a lively correspondence.

Atallah lit a cigarette, rested his head on the back of his seat, and exhaled smoke at the ceiling. After a while he cleared his throat and squeezed his esophagus in preparation for his speech. He nodded. "I am an admirer of your work, Nasif."

Nasif raised his gaze from his papers and directed it for a long moment at his guest, then said with a smile, "What work would that be, Atallah?"

"There is no longer any reason for secrecy. Hamdan sent me."

Nasif raised his eyebrows. "Really. And who is Hamdan?" he asked.

"You are a careful man. We thank you for that. The fate of many depends on the way you manage things and your sense of security. The fact is that Ismail Badr and his followers only met with their fate due to their impulsiveness and lack of caution. We can avoid this kind of thing if we are careful to avoid arrogance and do our work carefully and with secrecy."

Nasif sat on the edge of the desk, but stayed there only for a moment. He stood up quickly and paced the room restlessly. Finally, he came to stand in front of Atallah, arms crossed, staring at him calmly. Atallah began to feel some anxiety, as those eyes stared at him, trying to pierce the depths of his soul. He wanted to hide this anxiety and so he laughed awkwardly. "Am I under investigation?" he said. "Come now, Nasif, we have a huge task before us."

Nasif did not avert his gaze. In fact it became even sharper, as he asked, "What cell are you from?"

"My cell."

"Your superior?"

"You know I can't divulge that secret."

"Give me the letter."

Atallah removed an unsealed envelope from his pocket and handed it to Nasif, who unfolded it and read.

Dear Nasif,

The man who gives you this letter is trustworthy. He is an old freedom fighter who has suffered much for the movement. Please go with him as soon as you can to one Abdel-Aziz Mustafa, who is an employee in the Ministry of Interior. Do not write to me with the results of the meeting. I have left the residence you know, and have been away from Alexandria for a week. I will come to you soon, to speak to you about Mustafa and other matters.

Hamdan

The letter was not in Hamdan's hand, but the signature was close enough. Nasif studied it closely and then said, "Who gave you this letter?"

"What a question! I got it from Hamdan."

"Did he write it in front of you?"

"He gave it to me already written."

"Where is he now?"

"He asked me to keep that a secret. You know why."

"Did he ask you to keep it from me specifically?"

"I didn't ask. So, if you don't mind, I will keep it from you too."

"Strange. . . ."

Nasif struck another match and touched the flame to the letter. The flame consumed the paper, and he opened the window and held the smoldering remains outside, blowing on the ashes so they were carried away by the wind. While he was shutting the window, a violent banging echoed through the Citadel.

A shiver ran through Nasif's body. He froze in position. As Atallah looked at him, his face changed color, his face and lips slackened, his eyes widened, his arms fell by his sides. Seeing him like this, it was difficult to reconcile this pathetic, terrified specimen with the confident, arrogant Nasif who a moment ago had been pacing the room like a lion in his lair.

Sweat poured from his brow and his lips moved silently. He seemed to be on the verge of collapse, and leaned on the desk, muttering, "Who is it? Who . . . who is knocking . . . ? Malim! Malim! We are lost . . . lost. . . ."

And then, suddenly he was energized. He searched his pockets for something, and eventually pulled out a key with which he opened a drawer in his desk. He threw its contents all over the place, and finally found what he was looking for, yelling, "Here it is! I'll kill you, you filthy spy!"

Atallah leapt from his seat with an alarmed cry when he saw the gun in Nasif's hand pointed at his chest. This was particularly frightening, since the utter panic that had gripped Nasif made it not unlikely that this deadly tool would, in fact, fire at any moment. Atallah sought protection behind a bookshelf.

"Don't be crazy. Throw that gun away!"

But Nasif was advancing slowly. "I swear to you. If those are cops, they will only get to me over your dead body."

Atallah shrank behind his shelter and begged, "Be reasonable, man, by God! What do I have to do with the cops? You and I are in the same position!"

The banging began again, and Nasif trembled so violently he dropped his gun. Instead of picking it up, however, he began to wail. "What should I do? They will break down the door. . . . What is to be done . . . ?"

Atallah had a thought. He came out from behind the shelf and approached Nasif. "You have things that must not fall into the hands of the police, yes? Where are they?"

At that moment, they heard footsteps coming up the stairs. Nasif listened carefully, and stared intently at the door.

Atallah continued to urge him: "Quickly, before it's too late. Do you have copies of the last pamphlet you printed?"

But Nasif was not listening. He was frozen, eyes fixed on the door, as though expecting the appearance of an evil spirit. What good was doing anything now? All hope was lost.

The door burst open and Malim came in. "We're done for, Nasif Bey!" he said. "We're done for!"

A faint moan escaped Nasif's mouth. His eyes roamed the room as though searching for something. He collapsed into a chair. But he took a cigarette out of his pocket. He lit it with trembling hands. He ran his hands through his hair, and tidied it as best he could. Then he turned to Malim, and said in a quavering voice, "Let them come in. I am here. Long live Egypt."

# 12

As soon as those angry knocks reached Malim's ears, he left Haniya's room and rushed to the door. He stopped abruptly before reaching it, however, for he heard Khaled's voice asking the Madman about him.

What a catastrophe! He retraced his footsteps quickly, running to Nasif's room to plot a way out of this mess, but he found him performing a one-man political protest, in which he seemed to be supporting Egypt.

At the same time, he heard his father calling him from below. He did not know what to do. Quickly, however, he felt a complete disregard for the consequences, as he always felt when under pressure. He went down the stairs and asked him what he wanted.

"This effendi downstairs is asking for you."

The antechamber was lit only by a dim lamp, and Malim pretended to peer carefully to determine who the newcomer was, before finally exclaiming, "Why, Khaled Bey! Welcome. Please, do come in, Khaled Bey. All is well, I hope."

Khaled struck him with a piercing look. "You know exactly why I'm here."

"Why, Khaled Bey, how am I to know such a thing? Did my young mistress not keep her appointment with you?"

"What mistress, you lying hypocrite?"

"Strange. Did you not hear her voice on the phone?"

"Whose voice, you scam artist? Is this the honorable work you have always wanted?"

This discussion reached the Comrades, who were sitting around them in the dark, and Shatta said angrily, "Who is this, Malim? If he wants something, send him away. But cut his hands off first—he's given us all a headache with his damn knocking."

Malim said, with forced joviality, "This is Khaled Bey, Mr. Shatta. Please come through, Khaled Bey. Here you will find company that will make you feel better about your past."

Malim pushed him gently. Khaled found himself moving forward despite the fact that he was surrounded by the strangest group of young men he had ever seen. Malim introduced him. "This is Khaled Bey, whose father, the Pasha, sent me to the penitentiary."

Saad called out cheerfully: "Why hello, Khaled Bey. Have a seat. Your father is a bitter enemy to all of us."

Malim offered him a seat.

"Please sit. I will call the master of the house, to welcome you as you should be welcomed."

He ran back up to Nasif, and, finding that he had ended the protest, brought him up to date. Nasif had by this point reined in his emotions, and his confidence had returned. He was once more the master of the Citadel. He listened calmly to Malim, and, when he had heard the whole story, said curtly, "Bring him to me."

"He is very upset," Malim said, "and I fear—"

But Nasif interrupted him in his leader's way. "I said bring him to me."

"Wouldn't it be better if I called the Comrades too?"

Nasif frowned for a moment, and then said, "All right."

A minute later, the Comrades were gathered in Nasif's room, with Khaled at their center, amazed at what he was seeing. He was not expecting to find himself in such a strange setting. He had expected to see just Malim and his father in a humble house.

Nasif, in the meantime, had just lit another lamp, so that when Khaled entered he saw a bright light glowing from within, brightening every corner of the room. It was a spacious room, its furniture mostly oriental. On the right was a long couch, crafted in the Eastern style, and covered with a cloth of bright colors; on the left was a huge bookshelf draped with an elaborately decorated silk cloth. All over the room were benches with leather and silk cushions of the sort sold to tourists in Khan al-Khalili. In the center of the room was Nasif's desk, stacked high with books and papers of all kinds. Next to them was an antique gramophone, left by some ancestor or other.

But the only thing that caught Khaled's attention was a quote, written in English, hanging behind the man sitting at the desk. It was composed of three lines:

The great man is he who strives to create new things, new virtues.

The moral man is he who strives to keep everything as it is.

The greatest threat to the great man is that he become a moral man.


Nasif did not leave his chair when Khaled and the Comrades came in. He merely returned Khaled's greeting from behind his desk and pointed to a chair. Before Khaled could even open his mouth, Nasif turned to him and said that he was perfectly aware of the reason for his visit, and that he had no need to exert himself in attempts to prove his accusations, for they were all true. What Malim did, Nasif continued, was a scam, a means to make money. This was not theft, he pointed out, since although he had lost twenty piasters, he had received in exchange some lovely fantasies and joyful illusions, not to mention the pleasure of listening to a delicate feminine voice.

Khaled was tongue-tied. He didn't know quite how to respond. This was an exceedingly strange group of people. He was bewildered by what he was hearing and was not quite sure whether to admire these people or rage against them. Either way, his innate obstinacy drove him to disagree with Nasif's unusual opinions.

"I am not sure how Malim's actions could not be thievery. I didn't give him money to hear a delicate feminine voice, but to get something else I am sure you're familiar with."

Nasif leaned back and rested his head against the back of his chair, looking down at Khaled from his raised platform. "My dear Khaled," he said, "even if Malim had passed you on the road and lifted your wallet I would not consider it theft. Malim is poor. And it's not the poor who rob the rich, it's the rich who rob the poor of their bread, their health, and their happiness. They rob them of their very humanity. No, my dear Khaled, no. Suffice Malim his first experience. For it is your brother who was the thief. Your father who was the beneficiary. And it was Malim who paid the price."

Khaled liked what he was hearing. The only problem was that he was being placed in the same category as his brother and his father. This was upsetting, so he defended himself: "There may be some truth to what you're saying, but Malim did not scam my brother or my father. He scammed me. Me! His only defender. I, who left my own father and abandoned my family for his sake! Am I to understand that Malim has so lost his sense of dignity that—" But Khaled could not finish his soliloquy. He was interrupted by a sardonic laugh from Nasif.

"Did I hear you say 'dignity'? That's a word we are unfamiliar with here, my dear sir. The young men around you have chosen for themselves the name Comrade Bastards. Dignity! We have our own dictionary here, Khaled Bey. We call it the 'Dictionary of Poverty.' It has some words missing from it that you might be used to: dignity, honor, trustworthiness, and other ornaments that the rich can afford but that are a little expensive for the poor."

Now it was Khaled's turn to let out a mocking laugh. So he did.

"How strange. And here I thought that dignity and honor were gems that could only be worn by the poor. But now you tell me that the poor have no knowledge of such things. So can you tell me where to find them then?"

"Well, you could try the Department of Antiquities. You will find them with the mummies of the pharaohs. Right after the display with the weapons of the first conquerors and the detritus of the barbarians you read about in those history books. The new man doesn't need any of these fantasies, which only get in the way of his advancement. Dignity is just war. Honor is just jealousy and envy, followed by murder. As for trust, that's just theft. Because it is the primary tool for the one who stole to safeguard the loot he has stolen."

Saad stood up, yawned, and took a step toward Nasif, saying, "I don't think he understands anything you're saying. He seems to have been educated by some cavemen."

This made Khaled very angry. He was gripped by a great pride, and cried out, "Sir! I will have you know that I graduated from the most prestigious university in England."

Saad turned to Nasif. "Didn't I tell you? He's an illiterate." He turned back to Khaled. "My dear virtuous fellow. We don't trust university graduates here. No moral person could bear to remain in a university long enough to receive all the horseshit that is presented to him there. You really should have left school before you got your secondary school diploma. There is absolutely no excuse for your staying on any longer."

Shatta stirred. "Dignity! Really!" he said in a theatrical voice. "When I heard that word I felt like I was once more a little boy. I was about to ask this gentleman, Khaled, for a piece of chocolate." Standing up abruptly, he raised his hands. "Comrades," he said, "we must test Khaled to see if he is, in the first place, one of those people who is worth talking to or if we are simply wasting our breath. How about the Island Test? Agreed? Very well."

Shatta stuffed his hands into his pockets, walked toward Khaled, and then stopped. He looked at him for a moment. "Are you an islander, Mr. Khaled?"

Khaled raised his eyes and looked at his examiner. "I don't understand."

"Listen to me, Mr. Khaled. Let's pretend for a moment that you go on a trip with your family. While you are on the ship, in the middle of the ocean, a violent storm breaks and sinks the ship. Only two people survive. You and a sister of yours. You cling to the wreckage. You stay like this until the wind blows you onto a small island. When you have settled in, you explore it. You find out that there are no other humans but you and her. Days pass, and nights, and no one comes to save you. You are sure that you will never leave this place. Now, tell me, Khaled. Do you sleep with her?"

Khaled lost his temper. He jumped up from his seat and bellowed, "You mock me! You are using me for your own amusement!"

Atallah spoke for the first time. "Pay them no heed, Khaled Bey. They are always like this. If you want to leave, I am at your service."

Here, Nasif had to intervene. Speaking calmly, he said, "Relax, Khaled Bey. You seem to be a very sensitive person, which is a very serious failing, caused by these fantasies of dignity and pride which you indulge. It's a forgivable flaw, though, since it stems from an honestly mistaken under-standing of human nature. You imagine it to be a vast thing, embodying the whole of existence. Humanity is, for you, a sacred thing, owed some sort of obedience and respect. That's why you rage, and get uptight about the silliest things. But if you were just to go out to your balcony one evening and let your gaze wander over the uncountable planets and the stars, you would realize that the earth is simply a speck beside these gigantic worlds in the heavens. Then you would know that man is not just a contemptible thing, but that man is nothing. Nothing at all. It's like a piece of cheese, crumbled by the days, and with maggots crawling all over it. That's the earth. That's mankind."

Khaled could not bear this horrible image that Nasif had conjured. He bowed his head for a moment, frowning. Then he raised his head and asked, "If it's like that, then what is the point?"

Nasif shrugged. "There's no point," he said. "You are searching for something that doesn't exist. Like someone looking for a reason for the glitter of light on water. This earth we live on is just the result of some interactions that resulted in plants and cattle. If the temperature changed by one iota, or the earth was a little closer to or farther from the sun, you would see something else entirely, and none of these creatures would have the honor of seeing you. So where is the reason? What is the reason for there being no life on the moon? It's chance."

The Comrades continued their conversation. The first part of the night passed, and then the second, and still they talked and debated. They never tired of talking. Their thoughts manufactured meaning, their tongues spun phrases, and the states and destiny of the world spread out before them, and they could do with them what they pleased. Khaled was an opportunity to bring forth what was hidden in their minds, so they descended upon him and rained blows on him until the poor wretch became like a tennis ball knocked back and forth between their ideas, bewildered and awed.

Nasif led the charge. He was the final arbiter on every issue. Saad played the role of deputy. He handled secondary issues. He would explicate on these issues, providing commentary. Shatta, of course, looked at the speeches, and the speakers, from the theatrical perspective. This speech ended too quickly; this speaker didn't know how to use his voice to create the desired effect, and so on. Khoren always played a supporting role. Though he was the richest of the Citadel's denizens, there was a tradition among his comrades: they would leave him some remnants of their opinions for him to conclude. His conclusion was always: "There's no hope." He was like a secondhand seller, who made other people's leftovers into his own merchandise.

As for Atallah, as soon as he found out that Khaled was the son of Ahmed Pasha Khorshed, a man with a truly dangerous position in the Foreign Ministry, he gave Khaled his full attention. He sought to become his very best friend. Khaled had no champions among the group that night except Atallah, who sought to popularize Khaled's thoughts and defend them.

Early in the night, Haniya came in, and Khaled saw her for the very first time. So this was the woman with the enchanting voice that had echoed in his mind all day! She recognized immediately that Khaled had fallen victim to her enchantments, and she used her best weapons: large gray eyes; long curving lashes; easy laughter, delicate, like the ringing of wine glasses; and furtive glances that pulled at the lovestruck young man's heart.

That night, Khaled felt like he was in a dream. In his mind, a revolution of ideas. In his heart, a revolution of emotions. As for his self, he searched for it but couldn't find it.

And when dawn sent forth its first light, Khaled was opening the door of his room. He threw himself onto his bed and drowned in a sleep rich with dreams.

# 13

Events followed one another quickly after that night. The next day, Khaled rented a room in the Citadel. Ten days later, he was lying in the same jail cell where Malim had spent the night when he was accused of stealing that money.

The ideas whispered into Khaled's ears had a profound effect on him. At first he panicked. The ideas frightened him. He hated the idea that the world was as oppressively horrible as it was described by the Comrades. Despite this, however, he found himself accepting this image, and those ideas. He accepted the ideas when he realized they were simply the natural endpoint of the philosophy he had long ago adopted—the natural conclusion of the principles he had lived by, taken by the denizens of the Citadel to their inevitable end. But he had stopped in the middle of the journey and lit a pathetic little fire, more for the purposes of decoration than destruction. Now, though, he saw before him the red blaze of hellfire itself, with flames rising up on every side. He might as well throw himself into its embrace. There was no other way.

The Citadel's rooms were all taken, so they put him in the bathhouse next to Haniya's room. The bathhouse was spacious: floors and walls of granite, and its ceiling made entirely from stained glass in the Ottoman style that the Mamluks had adopted for their homes and clothes in their final days.

Most of the dwellers of the Citadel left in the morning to seek out their livelihoods. Often, the only people left would be Haniya and Malim, and occasionally Khoren. Khaled would spend his time in his room, ostensibly reading. The truth, however, was that he was unable to use his eyes for reading. He was too busy using them to stare at Haniya, through a hole in the door that separated them. Every moment that passed increased his infatuation. He couldn't think of anything but Haniya. He dreamt of her, and only her. Within three days, this state of passion had reached such a degree of tyranny, it became worship. The mere mention of her name induced a shivering in him that lit his heart with ecstasy and awe. He came to see anything that was connected with her as holy. He would scramble to the chair she had just left and, if no one was looking, he'd kiss the place where she'd been sitting. If there was someone in the room, he'd touch it gently with his fingers. At night, he would spend long hours, ears pressed to the door, listening to the sound of her breathing. He was so lost in love for her that he allowed himself once to enter her room in her absence and to take a handkerchief she had left lying on the bed. He would have taken the clothes from her wardrobe were it not for his fear that he would be found out.

The strangest thing about his state was that he professed an absolute contempt for women. What had fueled this feeling was that he was very attractive to many women of that class of people whose salons he used to visit until recently. He used to take pleasure in repeating to his friends that no one would ever catch him committing the crime of falling in love with a girl. Love, the way that most people understood it, was not real. It was an artificial construct, an illusion created by men who grew up in a society founded on ignorance and sexual repression. When the ignorance was lifted and the repression uncovered, love became just a form of calisthenics.

Haniya knew about Khaled's feelings. Usually, she was used to warding off the amorous advances of the Comrades. But with Khaled she took another approach. This was not because she had feelings for him, but because she felt a certain satisfaction at having this sort of effect on a young man who was somewhat different from the other young men in the Citadel. A young man who showed all the marks of wealth and comfort. A young man who was at home among that elite, which—despite all that was said about it—harbored a certain magic that bewitched those who did not belong to that class. And so she encouraged Khaled in his folly. She made it easy for him to think he could attain what he desired. She did all this with a subtlety that did not implicate her in any way.

Every night, Khaled heard opinions in the Citadel that were bold and revolutionary and seductive. He heard so many of them that at night they crowded his mind, babbling and confused, so he could not sleep. The person who had expressed this or that opinion intended only to amuse himself and pass the time. They were just inflated phrases repeated habitually to stimulate their minds and convince themselves that they were heroes in some epic.

The self, after all, needs to feel a little danger every now and then. Their ancestors, when they had that urge, would go out and duel or battle. Then people came up with the idea of sport, and satisfied that urge by watching cocks or bulls fight, watching boxing matches and football and other hidden barbarisms. As for the citizens of the Citadel, they invented this sort of talking duel, and stoked their blood-thirstiness during them. When the duel was done, their appetite for war and their desires were sated and they could sleep peacefully.

Khaled, unfortunately, thought of these verbal skirmishes as high truths that demanded hard work to actualize. Khaled had an earnest and loyal nature and he did not differentiate between words and convictions. He felt these thoughts with his very being, whereas they took it all as a means to exercise their tongues and listen to their voices. Khaled also thought that things would be easy, since no one in their right minds could object to reform, and the unjust could never withstand the power of a just cause.

That's why Atallah found in Khaled exactly the audience he was looking for: he filled his ears with speeches about the necessity of action. Enough talk! We need action. Decisive.

Immediate. He convinced him that the affair was easy, the path safe, the goal near.

And one night, discussion began in the Citadel and Nasif said, "The affair is difficult, the path hard, the goal is beyond our reach."

But Khaled objected. "What good does it do for us to talk among ourselves night after night? Our voices must reach the outside world, loud and clear, until they reach the ears of the government. Then they will make the reforms we demand!"

Haniya laughed and said, "All we are capable of over here, Khaled Bey, is talk. The decisive man, the man of action, has not come among us yet. If he were found, he would not need talk at all, given the amount of action he would need to make up for."

She sighed, and added, "Where is that man? He would raze this Citadel back to its foundations."

Nasif's face darkened. He was visibly upset by what he heard. He felt these jabs were directed at him personally, since he was the leader of the group and responsible for the guidance of its members. He flicked his cigarette away violently, and leapt into the fray.

"I'm afraid you simply don't understand," he said. "We limit our efforts to talk because that is our duty: to talk. The preceding generation was the generation that took the blows of injustice silently. Our generation is therefore the generation that must diagnose these problems. To express those injustices by talking. Our main role, our duty, is to work toward creating a social consciousness fully cognizant of these injustices, convinced of the need to correct them. This is our destiny. It is quite distinct from that role you consider the most noble of all because he who fulfills it gives his life as a service not to his own generation but to all the generations to come. He lives and dies an unknown soldier, unsung. If you see us talking, it is only so the next generation can work! The more we talk and study and discuss, the closer we are to our intended goal. You must be content with your destiny, Comrades! You must not shrink from the role that your destiny demands you fulfill!"

Usually, Khaled found Nasif's words deeply seductive. What gripped him on this particular night, however, were the words of that female object of his worship, which he felt were directed at him personally: "Where is that man?" He had to prove to her that he was the man she was looking for, that he was fashioned from a different clay than the other residents of the Citadel. How else could he aspire to her attention and affections, if he did not stand out? If he was to be worthy of her love, he had to rise to her level. Only then would she admire him. And so: action.

That night, the light did not go out in Khaled's room. Haniya felt him prowling around his room like a caged lion. She looked through the hole in the door and saw him poring over papers, examining them, and then tearing them up and pacing once more. By dawn, he was utterly exhausted.

He threw himself onto his bed and slept a disturbed and dream-ridden sleep, waking up every now and then in fear.

Early that morning he left his room and went looking for the Madman. His hair was uncombed, his beard too long, and his clothes were a mess, as though he had just arrived after a long journey. When he found the Madman, he talked to him for a while, and then took some papers out of his pocket. The Madman shook his head and smiled. Khaled insisted. The Madman refused firmly. Khaled pressed some money into his hand. The Madman's face changed. He accepted Khaled's offer.

A moment later, they both left the Citadel and did not return until the evening.

That night, Khaled sat with the Comrades, but he did not join them in their talk. They were blabbing and yelling as usual. As for Khaled, he took a seat at the edge of the group and observed them like a teacher observing his young students. He felt that he had done something that would distinguish him among them, that proved he was cut from different cloth. They were mere children, playing. Khaled was now a man, responsible, bearing dangerous burdens. The fate of many depended on him.

Haniya could sense that he looked at her strangely, and she did not understand it. He didn't seek her approval as he usually did. He didn't lose his composure when she glanced at him or spoke to him. He met her gaze coolly and with confidence, and responded evenly to her questions. In fact, he was a little haughty, as though things had turned around, and she was the one who was hopelessly in love. Haniya wanted revenge.

"Are you coming down with something, Khaled Bey?" she said to him.

Khaled looked at her a moment, and then said, "Why would you say something like that, Haniya?"

This was the first time he had ever spoken her name, and she worried that he would become too familiar with her, so she said quickly, "No reason. You just seem reserved. You haven't joined in the conversation."

Nasif laughed. "Maybe you won one of your court cases today," he said. "You seem drunk with victory and unconcerned with us or our conversation."

Khaled smiled, and said nothing. Atallah was watching him, and smiled a different sort of smile.

The next evening, Khaled snuck out of the Citadel, and if any of the Comrades had been there to see him they would not have recognized him. He was dressed in clothing quite unlike anything he usually wore: a long galabiya he had borrowed from Malim (with the excuse that his own pajamas needed washing) and a camel-wool cap on his head.

Khaled hurried down the road and did not notice that someone was shadowing him closely. He came to a café, and stood in front of it, hesitant. The person who was following him paused as well. Khaled had papers in his hands. He pushed them into his pocket and went into the café. The place was crowded and he took a corner and clapped to summon the waiter. When he came, Khaled asked for a hookah. He had never smoked a hookah before and so his first drag caused him to cough violently, which turned all the eyes in the room on him. He tried to cover his embarrassment. "Hey, man, is your hookah too hot or have I caught a sudden cold?"

One of the patrons laughed. "Bring him something warm and soothing, Mohamedein. That was a little rough on him."

Khaled turned to him, "Hey, we're all men here," he said, and clapped his hands. "Bring this good man a hookah. On me. Get a round for everyone on me. You're all my guests tonight."

Necks craned and eyes turned. Everyone took a look at this newcomer who volunteered to make them his guests, though they had no idea who he was. The room filled with muttering, mocking or surprised. Khaled in turn left his seat and stood among them. The clamor rose, and so did the laughter, and soon they had gathered around him tightly, with suspicion in their eyes. Khaled took the opportunity to jump up on a chair and yell at the top of his voice, "Brothers!"

Following this, there was a very long speech, which was incomprehensible to everyone in the room. It was, however, apparently very amusing, because the laughter of the patrons of the café only increased in volume. They heard him say that the peasants only ate a type of cheese called 'mish' and drank mud, and one of them asked him with a laugh, "Well, what do you want the peasant to eat and drink, baklava and tamarind?"

Khaled pointed out that the worker was mere prey to disease and that he was plagued with ignorance. "How is that any of your business?" one of them asked. And another suggested, "Just let him go. I think he is selling medicine or something. These pests have been showing up everywhere lately, even on the trains."

Finally, Khaled pulled the papers from his pocket and started to hand them out. "Read these pamphlets," he said, "and you'll understand what I mean. And say with me: Long live Egypt!"

"Oh, my God," one of them groaned. "What is this catastrophe that has descended on us in the middle of the night? Will someone please toss him out?"

But there was no need. The police invaded the café, arrested Khaled, handcuffed him, gathered the pamphlets Khaled had printed with the Madman's help, and led him off to the jailhouse, as the men laughed at him and the children taunted him.

When Khaled arrived at the prison they dragged him to the officer's desk and there, of course, he found his father. In fact, he found his father reclined comfortably and smoking a long, elegant cigarette. And, of course, in the corner, looking docile and with a vile smile on his lips, stood Atallah. There could be no doubt about it. He had fallen into a trap.

Ahmed Pasha raised his eyes and looked at his son for a long moment, and then said, with biting sarcasm, "I should have put those clothes on you myself, and lodged you with the servants. That would have taught you a well-deserved lesson. Hail! Hail, the conquering hero! We have been awaiting your glorious approach!" Then he turned to the police officer. "I hope, officer, that this investigation proceeds according to the book. Do not let this boy's relationship with me sway you in any way from carrying out the demands of justice."

The officer smiled. "I'm at your command, Pasha."

The interrogation lasted until after midnight, and then Khaled was deposited in a jail cell, where he spent the night with thieves and vagabonds. At one point he found himself weeping hot tears, his heart shattered by grief. At the moment when he had made up his mind to end his life, an old man came close to him and wrapped his arms around his shoulders.

"What's wrong, son?" he asked.

The old man spoke with a provincial accent that eased Khaled's heart. When he looked up at him he saw an ancient face, whose eyes glowed with loyalty and forgiveness. Khaled was in dire need of a gentle bosom to ease his burden. He asked the old man, "What brought you to this place, uncle?"

At this the old man laughed heartily. "It seems, son, that Cairo is out of bounds for the people of the countryside. I arrived here this afternoon, and had only taken a couple of steps on its streets when a man arrested me and charged me with vagrancy. That's all right, though. God will deal with him according to his intentions. And maybe they will let me go soon enough, who knows. As for you, son, we've heard a little about your story—"

Khaled interrupted him, eyes still streaming with tears. "What grieves me, uncle," he complained, "is that those who persecuted me, who mocked me, those who humiliated me so badly, were the poor! The poor, for whom I would spill my blood to the last drop, if it would bring them happiness."

The old man shook his head sadly. He put his arms around Khaled again. "What did you expect, my boy? The poor don't like to be called poor. You see, the fact is, the poor don't even recognize the existence of the rich from day to day. We have a whole world, complete in itself, and in this world all that exists are the poor. What do we care about the rich? They do not disturb us in any way."

Khaled had never heard anything like this. He thought about it for a while, then said, "You're right, uncle. The rich too have their own world, and the poor do not exist in it. Each of them walks on their own path, ignoring the other. I fear they will never meet."

# Epilogue

FOUR YEARS LATER, SAAD WAS strolling along in the neighborhood of Zamalek. The magazine he worked for had sent him to interview a former minister. When he knocked on the minister's door, he was informed that the minister was not home. The clock had almost struck nine, and he had nowhere particular to go, so he took from his pocket half a cigarette that he had saved for just such an emergency. He lit the cigarette and ambled along the dark alleyways.

All of a sudden, he heard the ominous scream of an air-raid siren. It was a scream that seemed both to invade the heart and to come from within the heart. It was now three years since the war had broken out, but it had been mere days since the air raids had started to follow one another like the flames of a fire. Not a day passed when these sirens did not scream, sometimes two, three, or even four times in a single night.

Saad told himself that he would not find somewhere to take refuge except if it became absolutely necessary. Being trapped in a small space with people, whose mouths gaped and eyes bulged, only increased his terror. Sometimes he thought it was the source of his terror. He raised his eyes and saw flashing swords of light, dueling in the sky, coming from all sides, so that the capital was covered with something like a fence made of light. It seemed to him almost as though Cairo were a basket, suspended by threads of light gripped in some heavenly hand.

But the raiding aircraft did not let him chase these fantasies. Their cursed whining sounded through the air, and was answered by the blasts of explosives. The sky was lit with brightly colored lights, and he ran.

It was his good fortune that he was near a shelter, and he rushed into it, aware of nothing but his need to seek cover. As he went through the door, he collided with a body that he recognized was a woman's only when he heard her voice, with its foreign accent, cursing him. He froze. "Haniya!"

A feminine voice replied, "Saad?"

"Yes!"

"Have you lost your mind, or just your eyesight?"

"Neither. Hurry, your people are taking it too far this evening."

Haniya turned to a shadowy figure behind her. "Let's go, my dear," she said.

Saad had beat her into the shelter, but when he heard her address someone, he stopped and turned. "Who's with you?" he asked.

She laughed. "Why, my husband, Mohamed Bey Salam."

Saad heard the voice of this venerable gentleman greeting him with a "Good evening, Saad Bey," and he cried out in surprise: "Malim! Come in. This is going to be one interesting party."

Saad had heard that Malim was occupied with some sort of business he carried out with the British army. This was at the beginning of the war. He then found out that his operation had grown, and that he now manufactured and supplied the Allied Forces with those badges sewed onto the uniforms of the soldiers. Most recently, the news had reached Saad that all this business had made Malim one of those notable wealthy men created by the war.

Saad had wondered why Malim would choose this sort of business, which would require a woman to oversee. He knew of course that Haniya had agreed to marry him, but he had also heard that it was a marriage of convenience, a way for Haniya to get her citizenship at a time when diplomatic relations with foreign countries were in danger of being severed completely. The proof that the marriage was in fact one of convenience was simply the fact that she had chosen Malim to be her husband. Malim who had been her servant.

But what he saw and heard this night showed him that this was no marriage of convenience. This was the marriage of a man to a woman who was madly in love with him, a woman who was utterly infatuated by her partner. Malim absorbed this love in his usual way, with silence and a smile. Malim hadn't become just any wealthy man. When he heard Haniya call him Mohamed Bey Salam, he knew that Malim was that same wealthy man who was the head of the Charity Cooperative, that philanthropist whose charitable contributions were the stuff of legend, reported on by the country's most prestigious papers.

The first question Malim asked, when they had settled in for the duration, was, "Where is Nasif?"

Saad shrugged and answered, "I don't know. He disappeared without a trace. No one sees him any more."

"I heard he was killed in an air raid in Alexandria."

"And I heard he married an old woman with some money and real estate."

Haniya laughed. "Those are the same thing."

The bombardment reached a frenzied peak. The caretakers of the shelter hissed at them to be silent. One of them said, "People, please. We want to hear what's happening outside."

Another added in fear, "That's a German plane. You can hear that rattling roar. God help us. We are Your servants."

Another outdid the first, making promises if he were to survive: "If you save me, O Lord, I will take back my ex-wife . . . ." and another responded with his own "And I will. . . ."

But the raiding planes had pitied the people their entanglements in oaths and promises that would get complicated in the near future. They departed, and their departure was met by applause from around the city of Cairo. The blasts of the antiaircraft artillery quieted down one by one, and a silence fell over the night, followed by a long whistle, which was met with wild and joyful applause.

The old Comrades emerged from the shelter and Malim headed to a grand, elegant automobile. Malim invited Saad to step into the vehicle. Saad hesitated at first, but what he had seen from Malim and Haniya soon soothed his pride. For yesterday's servant did not seem changed in the least by wealth. He was still the same modest, shy young man. He would have thought he'd encounter one of those young men who had only recently come into money. The kind of uncouth, vulgar people a gentleman could not bear to be around for a single moment. Malim seemed to feel that the money he had come into had forced itself upon him. He seemed to have yielded to this fate in the same way he had yielded to all the other twists of fate that had overcome him. As for Haniya, she had found a genuine confidence that made her even more beautiful, even more charming, than when she was poor and alone.

The three of them got into the car. Malim sat behind the wheel, and his wife sat by his side. Saad sat in the back seat.

The car moved with them through the dark streets, feeling its way cautiously, lighting its way with a dim blue light. Malim, as usual, was silent, speaking only if asked a question. Haniya was glowing with love for her husband and her life. She could not be silent, and regaled Saad with tales of their journeys and vacations, of their elegant mansion overlooking the Nile.

"But more beautiful than all that," she said to him, "is Malim Junior. He is a rare treasure and his beauty will overwhelm you when you see him."

"Not surprising," Saad replied, "if Haniya gave birth to him."

"But he doesn't look like me at all! He is the exact copy of his father."

And she began to extol the virtues of the child—his good humor, his wit, and so on—until Malim laughed and silenced her with an old expression: "Easy there, you're disturbing his sleep."

Silence reigned, until Malim broke it with a question: "How are the rest of the Comrades, Saad? I don't see them around."

Saad sighed. "Me neither, my friend. The only one I see is Shatta. And that is only because I am still a journalist and he still works for his Jewish broker. It's as if our destinies have forgotten us. They have left us where we were, but they have played with the lives of our comrades in strange ways. Has the news of Khoren reached you?"

"What happened to him?"

"He was overcome by the wiles of some Jezebel. She conned him out of his late father's fortune. He took it well, though. He laughs about it. He keeps saying, 'This is justice— the money from those Armenian shoes my father made must have been ill-gotten gains.'"

"What's he doing now?"

"You're not going to believe this, but he works as a salesman in one of those big stores."

Haniya laughed. "What a disgraceful student! I didn't know he would so totally degrade the art I taught him."

Saad couldn't help himself. "Well, Haniya, it seems to me that art is what disgraced him in this way. Were you not teaching him surrealism? This department store he works for, with all those random things, all those manifold things, is the truest expression of that art."

Haniya whipped her head around threateningly. "Are we going to have this fight again?"

Malim smiled. "Why don't we leave surrealism in peace, Saad? I have it hanging over me at all times. Tell me, do we know anything about Atallah?"

"Atallah's fate, now that is a strange and wonderful thing. His is the strangest fate of all."

"Did he leave his job with the secret police?"

"He was fired two days after Khaled's arrest. It was the only request that Khaled made of his father after their reconciliation. You know what he did, this man who spied on revolutionary movements for the police?"

"What did he do?"

"He started a revolutionary movement. You can find him now camped out at the Egyptian University, roving among the students, driving them to delusions, recruiting them for his movement. What's even more unbelievable is that he's now setting up a publication to express his ideas."

Haniya shook her head. "What a weird gang. I look at my life then, and it all seems like a dream."

Silence reigned again, but this time it was a pregnant silence, because the couple had asked about all the Comrades except one. It was easy to ask about Nasif and the rest of them. As for that other young man, he had a different nature. It was impossible to know him without that knowledge leaving a strange trace in the soul. He was not like the rest of them. He was not just a mind that thought and a tongue that spoke. He was blazing emotion, gushing sentiment, contagious, bringing others to feverish feeling. You loved him or you hated him, or you had some mysterious feeling that was love and hate at once and might just be anger. Because in the end he made you feel how you really felt about things. And no one can tolerate that for very long.

But now here they were. There was nothing to do but ask about that other young man. The question filled the air. It was clear in the faces of the couple that even they could not bring themselves to ask it.

At last Haniya said in a quiet voice, "I heard you say that Khaled made up with his father."

"Yes. Didn't you know that?"

"No. When did it happen?"

Saad laughed sardonically. "When did it happen? Well, my dear, it happened the very day he was arrested. He didn't stay in prison longer than that one night."

Haniya shook her head. "How strange. I would have expected that from anyone but him. How could someone change their very nature so quickly, overnight?"

Saad was silent for a while, and then said, "Maybe it was excusable. One man can't fight the whole world. Especially if he gives himself over to his feelings like Khaled did. The crime he was arrested for was broad, and could have been prosecuted as a serious offense or been seen as negligible and be dismissed. His father explained this that morning and gave him the choice. The price for not pressing charges was that Khaled drop all his lawsuits against his father and be a loyal son. Khaled paid the price."

"So," Haniya said, "he sold himself to the devil."

"Have you not seen him since that night?"

"No."

"Well then, let's go see him tonight. He's usually at some grand place surrounded by the other sons of very rich men. You can judge for yourself the kind of deal he made with the devil."

Haniya turned to her husband. "Do you mind, my dear?"

Malim shook his head. "Not at all, Haniya."

The car had already passed the city limits of Cairo, but they turned back.

There was no one home at the grand place when the three of them arrived. Malim looked around but could find no trace of Khaled. Saad gestured for them to follow him. He walked toward the stairs at the far side of the room, and they went up to the upper floor. There, in a solitary corner, they saw the back of a young man facing a brazen woman inserting the pipe of a hookah into her mouth, as clouds of smoke wafted above her head. Save for the fact that he had gained a little weight, the young man looked like Khaled. But Malim and Haniya sensed that something strange had happened to him, and that they did not know him any more. His full neck suggested an animal appetite and a sense of profligacy. His lounging posture was decadent, and somehow lacking in vitality.

There was no one on that floor but Khaled and his female companion, so when he heard their footsteps he turned around lazily. He looked at them for a long time without seeming to recognize them. After a while, he turned back around, raised his glass, and took a sip.

Haniya almost cried out when she first saw Khaled's face. She had known that face long ago, and it had been like a child's face, gentle and clear, so that one could see every ripple caused by the young man's heart. But now he seemed to have placed a mask over that face. It was as if he had borrowed the visage of one of his savage ancestors who roamed the forests and ate human flesh. The hateful creases around his mouth and the dark glow of his lustful mad eyes frightened her.

Something in her told her to retreat.

She leaned in and whispered something to her husband, but Saad said to her softly, "Don't be afraid. He doesn't bite."

He came close to Khaled and stretched out his hand. Khaled, startled, peered into the face of the man greeting him. "Saad . . . ?"

Without rising from his chair, he shook Saad's hand and said sharply, "Sit."

Saad, still standing, asked, "Where are the rest of your companions?"

"The raid took them in its wake. Sit."

"I have two guests with me. You'll be surprised to see them."

Khaled looked bored, and spoke with some irritation. "Nothing surprises me any more. Go tell them that you couldn't find me. Or that I was killed in the raid. Tell them anything you like as long as you can come back without them. Can't you see that I have a woman I've been plying with wine all day, so that I can have her all night?"

Malim's honor rejected such talk. His jaw clenched and a fire blazed in his eyes. This grim, intense man was the one who inspired so much love in Haniya, and she clung to him even more closely and smiled in admiration of her husband. But Malim pushed her away from him firmly and stepped toward Khaled.

"Good evening, Khaled Bey."

Khaled looked at the speaker with disdain. "Hello, sir. Is there something I can do for you?"

Malim did not seem bothered by this attitude. He spoke with confidence. "I am Malim. Haniya, my wife, and I came to greet you."

What a catastrophe! This was the voice of the past that Khaled had been trying to silence with hundreds of glasses of wine and dozens of women. And there he was, hearing it again. It assaulted his ears. It said, "I am Malim." Malim, who was the axis of his old life. Malim, who was the symbol of all that was noblest in him. Malim, who had slipped through his grasp for the last four years. And there he was before him. Malim, Khaled's conscience given human form, who had come to see him in his present state.

But Khaled was drunk. After all, he had spent four years doing nothing but murdering, with premeditation, everything that Malim represented in him, everything that Malim meant. And so he succeeded in reining in his feelings. He succeeded in putting on that hateful mask that had so frightened Haniya. He said to himself, "Did the three of them not come to see Khaled engaged in some cheap decadence? Let us not disappoint them. Let Khaled perform."

He got up lazily and shook Malim's hand, as if bored. "Malim? Don't you mean Mohamed Bey Salam? I know everything about you."

He turned to Haniya and spoke to her as if seeing her for the first time. "Have a seat, my lady."

They all sat. No one knew what to say. At last Khaled spoke, ironically, in a careless tone. "I think the lady Haniya and Mohamed Bey are astonished to see me in this state."

Haniya curled her lip and echoed his words. "Nothing surprises me any more."

Khaled gave a smile almost identical to his father's hateful smile. He spoke slowly. "I beg you not to mock me, my lady. I am just a simple man but I am now a sane one. And all this sanity has made it clear to me that obedience to our fathers is the only way for sons to be happy. For example, it allows me to refer to my father as 'Baba Pasha.' This in turn opens all kinds of doors. It allows me to live the most profligate life I am capable of living, and without anyone ever holding me to account. My pockets are absolutely saturated with money. The doors of the houses of the grandest families are thrown wide open for me. People pray in my wake, 'May God bless this obedient son.' What more do you want from me?"

Haniya shook her head and said, sighing, "More than what, Khaled Bey?"

Khaled lost his sense of irony for a second. For a moment he had his old face again. He said, in a sad voice, "Please just let me be, my lady."

But then he raised his head and spoke forcefully, "Don't you dare hold me responsible for this state. I am merely the victim of my generation. This is the most miserable age since God created the world. You will not find a single person who is conscious of the world he lives in and is at the same time capable of joy. Why, you ask? It's all this damned cleverness. Human cleverness has gotten far beyond our capacity for true knowledge, for experiential knowledge. You could call it the wisdom of being if you like. Because knowing is not just a matter of simple cleverness. It is cleverness and a physical body, or example. We now know things with our minds only, but we don't know how to know things with our whole being, with our joy and our pain, with our bodies. Our bodies are still caught in the old ways of knowing. Still tied with the chains of selfishness and greed and jealousy and murder and superstition. Delusions that have overcome entire nations.

"So, what do you expect from someone who is shackled by all these chains, even if his mind knows how stupid they are? You can only expect what you see before you. I can't untangle these bonds until the whole society I live in frees itself from the same bonds. And they can't unravel these chains unless each person's intelligence is at one with their whole being. And this will take many generations. Don't be amazed when I tell you that civilization is going through its strangest phase. It used to be that a man could reach a spiritual joy by mortifying his flesh, by denying himself worldly joy. In this way, intelligence could rise to become the wisdom of being. No wonder: that wisdom was always seeking to reach the highest peak. Even the ancient Egyptians had gods, and those before them had other gods. This wisdom produced laws and applied them, permitting some things and forbidding others. Cleverness back then was an animal thing, ruled by the laws of the jungle, and the wisdom of being was higher than it, and more noble.

"Today we have the opposite problem. It is cleverness that has reached the highest peak: transcendent and creative, respecting no limits, fearing no authority and no power. And wisdom, the wisdom of being, of being whole, is failing. Its own laws have been used to imprison it. If a man wants to find joy now, he must go back to being an animal. This is what I have done. I cannot singlehandedly raise the wisdom of being of an entire nation to a level capable of competing with the cleverness of those other nations of the world. All I have left in my power is to hide behind this mask that inspires such fear in you. But that fear is unfair. Have you never read that line: 'You look to the heights when you seek joy, but I look to the depths'? That is the situation of every intellectual in this damned age. We have to sink to the depths."

The words were pouring out of Khaled, chasing one another. They seemed well rehearsed. When he had finished, silence returned for a long time. As for Haniya, toward whom this soliloquy was directed, her eyes had flooded with tears.

At long last, Saad broke the silence. He shook his head and sighed. "Oh, you Egyptian Hamlet, always so full of confusion."

Khaled glanced at him in despair. "Oh, Egypt," he replied, "always burying your head in the sand."

SELECTED HOOPOE TITLES

*The Egyptian Assassin*
by Ezzedine C. Fishere, translated by Jonathan Wright

*Clouds Over Alexandria*
by Ibrahim Abdel Meguid, translated by Kay Heikkinen

*The Hashish Waiter*
by Khairy Shalaby, translated by Adam Talib

\*

**hoopoe** is an imprint for engaged, open-minded readers hungry for outstanding fiction that challenges headlines, re-imagines histories, and celebrates original storytelling. Through elegant paperback and digital editions, **hoopoe** champions bold, contemporary writers from across the Middle East alongside some of the finest, groundbreaking authors of earlier generations.

At hoopoefiction.com, curious and adventurous readers from around the world will find new writing, interviews, and criticism from our authors, translators, and editors.